An Unlucky Moon

By Carrie Ann Ryan

An Unlucky Moon

A Dante's Circle Novel

By: Carrie Ann Ryan

Published by Fated Desires Publishing, LLC.

© 2013 Carrie Ann Ryan

ISBN: 978-1-62322-038-9

Cover Art by Scott Carpenter

Dedication

To Marie Harte.

Thank you for being crazier than me. Maybe.

Acknowledgments

First, thank you to Lexi Blake, Marie Harte, Cari Quinn, and Jayne Rylon. You know why.

A huge thanks goes to my team of editors, assistants, and crew. Devin, Donna, Vickie, Fatin, Lillie, and Kelly—thank you for helping make *An Unlucky Moon* what it is. You guys do so much work for each release and I know I couldn't do it without you.

Also, thank you to my Street Pack and Fan Club. You guys work so hard at getting the word out and I am so blessed for it.

Thank you, Lia, for being my BFF, writing buddy, chat addict, and...everything.

And thank you to my readers. I get to do the best job in the world because of you.

Thank you.

Dante's Circle Characters

With an ever growing list of characters in each book, I know that it might seem like there are too many to remember. Well don't worry; here is a list for you so you don't forget. Not all are seen in this exact book, but here are the ones you've met so far. As the series progresses, the list will as well.

Happy reading!

Agda—Brownie council leader.

Agnes—Sole female on the Angelic council.

Amara Young—One of the seven lightning struck women. Works at an inn. Has a past that is very secretive.

Ambrose Griffin—Warrior angel, Shade's mentor. Father to Laura *(deceased)* and Nathan *(deceased)*, husband to Ilianya *(deceased)*. Mate to Balin and Jamie, story told in *Her Warriors' Three Wishes*.

Azel—Black-winged angel. Striker's third in command.

Balin Drake—Non-soul devouring demon, son of Pyro. Mate to Jamie and Ambrose, story told in *Her Warriors' Three Wishes*.

Becca Quinn—One of the seven lightning struck women. Works as a bartender at Dante's Circle. Mate to Hunter Brooks, story told in *An Unlucky Moon*.

Bryce—Lily's ex-fiancee.

Caine—Angelic council leader.

Cora—Shade's ex-fiancé *(deceased)*.

Dante Bell—Dragon shifter. Owner of Dante's Circle.

Eli—Bakery Owner.

Eliana Sawyer—One of the seven lightning struck women. Works as a welder.

Faith Sanders—One of the seven lightning struck women. Works as a photographer.

Fawkes—Demon, son of Lucifer, friend of Balin. Story told in *His Choice* (Found in the Anthology *Ever After*).

Fury—Leader of the demon council.

Glenn—Lily's sleazy ex-boss.

Hunter Brooks—Wolf and Beta of the Nocturne Pack. Met Ambrose, Jamie, and Balin in hell during the demon games. Mate to Becca, story told in *An Unlucky Moon*.

Ilianya—*(deceased)* Sister to Shade, wife to Ambrose.

Jamie Bennett—One of the seven lightning struck women. Bookstore owner and lover of romance. Mate to Ambrose and Balin, story told in *Her Warriors' Three Wishes*.

Kobal—Old djinn council member, ally to Pyro.

Law—Gray-winged angel, Striker's second in command.

Lily Banner—One of the seven lightning struck women. Worked as a lab chemist in solid-state NMR. OCD and quirky. Mate to Shade, story told in *Dust of My Wings*.

Lucifer—Infamous demon from hell and Fawkes' father.

Laura—*(deceased)* Daughter of Ambrose.

Nadie Morgan—One of the seven lightning struck woman. Works as a school teacher.

Nathan—*(deceased)* Son of Amborse.

Pyro—Demon from hell, father to Balin.

Shade Griffin—Warrior angel, ex-fiance to Cora, brother to Illianya, mate to Lily Banner, story told in *Dust of My Wings*.

Striker—Angelic council member, leader of the rebels.

Temperance—New Djinn council leader.

Thad—Co-worker of Lily's. Had a crush on him.

Timmy—10 year old brownie.

reigns."

"For now," Dorian Masterson whispered, though Hunter wasn't sure if anyone else had heard the bastard.

Hunter had keener senses than most wolves due to his bloodline and destiny. His stint in the gladiator games of hell had only honed them stronger. He'd been back only a month, and he still didn't feel as though he fit in his skin. Everything had changed in his absence.

The council had grown with more power. His Alpha had grown weaker without Hunter there to protect him. Josiah's last protector had perished

Samuel...Samuel, Hunter's brother, had died protecting the Alpha when the council had tried to take over.

None of it made sense to Hunter. He'd fought for his life countless times and killed so many demons and other supernaturals that he wasn't sure the blood would ever leave his hands, yet when he'd returned to the human realm, he'd faced another battle.

His own Pack.

Hunter rolled his shoulders then stalked toward his Alpha, who stood surrounded by the five council members. That alone pissed him off to no end. The council should have no place near the Alpha. There were only advisors on good days and whispers on bad ones.

Yet they stood there and had demanded a fight to the death to secure the position of Beta.

A position that Samuel had held.

A position Hunter had held before he'd been taken by the demons and forced to serve.

He knelt in front of his alpha, glaring at the others as he did so.

"My Alpha," Hunter grumbled then turned his head to the side to bare his neck. Others gasped around him, but he ignored them. They *should* have been the ones to bare their necks, but they'd become lax in their duties and rituals.

They'd thought the Pack was a democracy.

They would soon be proven wrong.

Josiah put his hand on Hunter's shoulder and nodded. "You're a fine Beta, Hunter. You will make me proud. You *make* me proud."

Something warm started to fill him, piercing through the ice at his Alpha's words, then dissipated. His wolf howled within him and hardened against the intrusion. No, it wouldn't do any good to warm at his Alpha's words.

Hunter wasn't a warm man. He was a killer—his Alpha's killer. He'd been raised to be that wolf, and he'd fulfilled that promise in hell. Now he was back within the confines of his Pack and ready to kill again.

Or at least that's what he told himself.

"Hunter, good fight," Alec Brennan, another of Hunter's one-time friends and council member, said as he slapped his shoulder. "You almost killed that Lloyd wolf." A vicious gleam entered Alec's eyes, and Hunter grunted.

"Let the wolf live in his memory of defeat," Hunter growled. "I'm not in the mood to kill a useless slug who isn't worthy of the title Beta."

"Watch what you say about my son," Gregory Lloyd snarled. The older council member tried to come at him, his teeth bared, but Alistair Jacobs—the remaining council member—held him back.

"It would do no good to fight like animals," Alistair drawled. "We might have the wolves at our beck and call, but we *will* remain civilized."

Hunter snorted at that. There had to be over a hundred wolves surrounding them in human form, each shirtless, ready to shift if necessary. Each adult male—and some of the juveniles—were marred with scars and tattoos that celebrated their victories in battle.

At any moment, since the circle was over, they could break out in brawls to release the tension.

There were only two ways to release the tension riding through their bodies—fighting and sex. As wolves, they didn't care about privacy and modesty. If there was a woman—or a man, if that was their inclination—in front of them, they'd fuck them hard, letting the stress and worries from the day seep away.

Since there were no willing partners at the moment, Hunter was sure a fight would break out soon. Blood and sweat would soon permeate through the air, filling Hunter's nostrils to override the stench of betrayal and anger that poured from the wolves that had lost their hope today.

Today, like most other days, fighting would rule over sex.

The females were back in their homes—what few females they had. Wolves were born, not bitten, in their world, unlike what the fandoms believed. Though it was easy to get pregnant, it was hard as hell to keep that baby and even harder to produce a girl.

Their absence at the circle meeting had been the council's decision, not the Alpha's. Their history had always held their women in deep respect. Not only were they wolves in their own right, but strong fighters as well. They were feared among the men if someone threatened their pup.

Yet the council had declared them weak in Hunter's four-year absence. Apparently the women—and men—who had fought back against the council taking over had been beaten or killed.

Nothing was right in the Nocturne Pack.

Hunter kept blaming the council for all of it, but he knew it wasn't the five of them. No, it was three of them who held the power—or at least thought they did.

For now.

"Come on," Liam whispered. "Let's look at those cuts of yours at my place. It will rain soon anyway. I'd prefer not to get my hair wet." He grinned at his last remark, but Hunter didn't respond. Unspoken was their need to talk about the undercurrents within the circle.

Hunter had been back in the human realm for a full month, yet change took time. After Ambrose, Jamie, and Balin—

and of course the young demon, Fawkes—had rescued him from the depths of hell, he'd returned to the realm he'd grown up in.

Unlike most supernaturals, wolf shifters and some other types of shifters lived within the human realm but were hidden deep within the forests. Their own magic kept the humans away and their secrets buried. Other supernaturals lived in other realms that were accessible through only the human realm. It was as if the humans themselves were the glue that held everyone together.

Fitting considering the humans weren't really humans at all but merely diluted down versions of supernaturals themselves. They didn't know the things that went bump in the night were real and had no idea that, within themselves, they held the ability to change into another being...if something were to alter their course, that is.

Hunter had grown up with the humans around him and his Pack at his side. They might be dark and depraved in the best of times, but he'd loved them like his own.

He'd thought he'd return to the Pack he'd known, but that had not been the case.

Four years was a long time to be gone.

Everything had changed and not for the better. Though one thing might offer the light on his horizon.

He'd left her alone so he could find his place and be better for her. Now it was time.

He'd find her soon. His Becca.

"You must be thinking about a woman," Alec teased as they made their way back to Liam's home. "You're smiling."

Hunter grunted then walked inside the place with Liam and Alec following. He turned on the lights and stretched his arms over his head. He was damned tired after that run even though he still felt a bit on edge since he hadn't hunted big game.

"I don't smile," Hunter growled.

Alec just shook his head and stole a beer from Liam's fridge. Liam scowled and slapped the back of Alec's head.

"You never ask to take my shit," Liam snapped.

Alec frowned. "I didn't think I had to, Murray," he drawled.

Hunter blinked at the two of them, their tension different than it had been before he'd been gone. While before the two had always bickered and annoyed each other, this felt different. Before they'd always smile and get over it, the tension dissipating after a few moments. Now, though, there seemed to be an underlying current between the two that Hunter couldn't quite put his finger on.

"Guys? It's beer. Get over it."

The two men swiveled their heads at him and glared. They might have looked nothing alike, Liam with his dark looks and blue eyes, Alec with his brown hair and green eyes, but right then, they had the same expression.

Hunger, anger, and confusion all rolled into one.

What the hell?

Looking at Liam, Alec twisted off the beer cap then took a long swig. Liam's jaw clenched as he ground his teeth together, and then he handed Hunter a bottle.

Hunter looked between the two men but put his questions aside. He had enough to deal with without delving into whatever drama they had.

"Tell me about what I missed," he said after a minute of awkward silence.

"Everything, Hunter," Liam said.

"No shit," Hunter snapped. "Give me specifics."

"When you left—" Alec began then cut himself off. The other man clenched his jaw then took a deep breath. "No, when you were *taken*, things went to shit. We still don't know how you were taken to the demons, Hunter. You have to believe that."

Hunter nodded and meant that. He knew the two men in this room wouldn't have sold him to the demons. That was all he knew though. He had his ideas of what had happened, but no proof.

Finding out how he'd been sold as a slave to the highest

demon bidder was high on his list of priorities.

Liam cleared his throat then put his hand on Alec's shoulder before sitting down on the couch. Alec shot him a look, and Liam pulled his arm away.

"When you left, Masterson, Lloyd, and Jacobs thought they found an opening for their plan," Liam continued. "They've never hidden from those who've looked as though they want to take over the Pack. They want to bring the wolves into the twenty-first century, as they put it, and force a democracy."

Hunter cursed. "We're wolves. That cannot happen. None of the other Packs who have tried that have survived. We're not humans. We have wolves wrapped around us, deep within the very aspects of our souls and beings. Denying an Alpha should hurt."

Liam nodded. "You're not telling us anything Alec and I haven't said before. The amount of pain, though, depends on the Alpha."

Hunter held back a grimace. "Josiah is getting older, but we don't age like humans. His power should only increase with age."

Alec shook his head. "Not without a Beta who can support him or without the magics that got him the position anyway. An Alpha can't survive without a Beta. Josiah holds all the magic and strength of the entire Pack on his shoulders, but he can't rule and be himself without another to lean on."

Hunter nodded. "He would have been fine if he hadn't lost Clara."

Liam ran a hand through his hair. "She's been gone for a decade, Hunter. Josiah is stronger than he gives himself credit for, but he can't do it alone. He shouldn't have to do it alone."

"And Samuel, may he rest in peace, wasn't strong enough to protect him," Alec whispered.

Hunter didn't wince or move at the mention of his late brother's failures. No, that wasn't quite right. He couldn't call his brother's decision a failure since the boy had done all in his power to protect the Pack. It just hadn't been good enough.

There had never been any question that Samuel hadn't been strong enough for the position, but the kid should never have been put in harm's way to begin with. If Hunter had been there, Samuel would be alive.

That above all else would be something that would haunt Hunter until the day he died.

"Have you found his killer?" Hunter asked, his voice low, deadly.

Alec shook his head. "No, but we can make guesses."

"The three bastards who think they can take over the Pack." Hunter clenched his fists, his fury riding him hard.

"You're here now and named Beta in truth," Liam said. "We couldn't do it alone, not and keep our families alive and the Pack fluid, but we'll be by your side, Hunter."

Hunter nodded but stayed silent.

"The struggle has only just started, Hunter," Alec put in. "We don't know what the others have in store, and we don't know exactly what they've done in the past. All we know is that we'll protect Josiah and you with our lives."

Hunter inclined his head at the two men who had been his best friends since they were pups. The three of them had always been thick as thieves, and when they'd grown into adult wolves, they'd taken their positions as council members and Beta in stride.

Alone they were strong.

Together they were stronger.

"This will cause a war if we're not careful," Liam murmured.

"We're already in a war," Hunter said flatly. "We just need to make sure it's contained."

The last thing he wanted was to bring their conflict into the other realms and hurt the humans.

Especially one particular human. She'd already been hurt once from a supernatural battle, and he'd be damned if he'd let another touch her.

He'd walked away from her once to ensure her safety.

He wouldn't do it again.

Chapter Two

Okay, you bastard, stay where you are," Becca Quinn snarled at her enemy. She gripped her weapon and planted her feet, ready to take on the foul creature, even if it meant endangering her life.

It was past time for this bastard to die.

Her enemy twitched, but otherwise looked nonplussed.

"I won't let you win this time," she vowed. "You and your little friends might have won before, but not this time. Today I'll be the victor, and you'll be the one writhing in pain, helpless and screaming."

Images of gold eyes and the faint sound of a wounded howl filled her mind, but she pushed those away.

It wasn't the time.

"Becca, kill the damn spider and get on with it," Dante Bell, her boss and friend, barked from the doorway.

Becca groaned but didn't let her gaze fall from her fierce enemy. The eight-legged nightmare that had to be as big as her hand merely lifted a leg as if he hadn't a care in the world.

He probably didn't.

She quickly looked at the plunger in one of her hands and bottle of bleach cleaner in the other. Fine, she might have gone overboard with her weapons of choice, but considering she was in the bar bathroom, she took what she could get.

"He could kill me at any moment," Becca said.

"He's a spider, Becca," Dante growled. "A spider. You've seen demons, angels, and heard of who knows what else, and you're afraid of a measly spider."

Becca snorted. "He could be a spider shifter for all we know, ready to kill me as soon as I relax."

"For the gods' sake. There are no such things as spider shifters. Don't even think about asking me to kill if for you, Becs. Get a damn shoe."

Becca finally pulled her gaze from her enemy and turned to glare at Dante. "You'd sit back and let me die?"

Something dark passed through his piercing blue eyes, and he set his jaw. She blinked as she remembered that her friend and boss wasn't human. His long black and blue hair, his tattoos and piercings, and everything else about him hid who he was.

The dragon within him, the one she and her friends had never seen, was right under the surface.

Waiting.

"I'd rather walk through the fires of hell, the same hell I'm banned from, then sit back and watch any of you girls die. You know this. I'm standing back and letting you kill the fucking spider because you asked me to, Becca Quinn. You told me you wanted to face your fears, and I'm letting you. Never forget what I am and never forget that I'd die before watching you or the girls get hurt."

With that, he turned on his heel and left her alone in the bathroom, her heart in her throat and her shame surrounding her.

Hell, she'd fucked that up.

Badly.

She turned back to the corner, only to find it empty. Panicked, she scanned the walls, floors, under the stalls, and her hair, only to come up short. The damned arachnoid-of-death had eluded her.

He and all his little friends would be back though, and she'd be ready.

Maybe.

She put the plunger and bleach back under the counter

and washed her hands. It wasn't as though she could spend hours chasing after something that probably wouldn't hurt her when she had to go back to work and be a perky waitress.

Becca groaned then put her curly mass of red hair back into its semblance of a ponytail. Her body ached something fierce, and she really didn't want to put a smile on her face and pretend that she loved her job.

Well, that wasn't really fair. She loved meeting new people, and she loved Dante like the big brother she'd never had—the hot-as-hell big brother—but it wasn't as if she was attracted to him beyond a glimpse of hotness.

No, she had another man in mind when it came to whom she wanted. Not that she'd seen Hunter in a month.

No, he'd left her high and dry after saving her life in the alley when a man attacked her. Then Hunter had been there when she'd almost died in the attack from the djinn.

Hell, her life didn't sound real anymore. She used to be the unlucky one of the group, which included her and her six friends. She was always tripping over something or tearing a hole in her shirt by just standing against a wall or something.

Then lightning had struck her and her friends, literally, and everything had changed.

Becca snorted. Didn't that just sound like something out of a horror novel?

They'd all survived, Dante as well, though she didn't find out until later *why* he was unharmed. After all, a dragon had to have thick scales, right?

Since that night when the room had lit up like a Christmas tree and her body had filled with a manic form of energy, things had been different. Lily had been the first to notice the change when she'd met Shade, a warrior angel from the angelic realm. He'd been there to stop her from finding out that the supernaturals existed, but it had all been for naught.

Since Lily and Shade were true halves, once they, ahem, *connected* on a deeper level, Lily had changed into a supernatural creature in her own right—a brownie. It seemed that the not-so-human part of her DNA had become dominant.

The same thing had happened a year later with Jamie, though she'd changed into a djinn. Her transformation hadn't been as beautiful as Lily's though. The demons of hell had taken her to their own realm and had almost killed her. Thankfully Shade's mentor, Ambrose, had risked his own life to save her. There they'd met the third of their triad, Balin, and lived to tell the tale. Becca still couldn't believe that little bookstore owner Jamie was in a ménage relationship in which Balin and Ambrose were also lovers.

From the way her friend always blushed and glowed, Becca figured things were working out.

It had been only a month since everyone had come back to the human realm and they'd defeated the demon and djinn who'd wanted to harm them. Becca herself had almost died by being impaled by a piece of wood. Jamie had saved her body, but it had been Hunter who'd saved her soul.

She'd known from that instance that Hunter would mean something more to her than just being a stranger who'd saved her in a dark alley. She'd seen the pain and anguish within those gold eyes and had heard his howl. That had brought her back while Jamie had healed her wounds.

Then Hunter had left to go back to his Pack, and Becca was stuck working at the bar with Dante, wondering why she cared about the wolf who hadn't looked back.

A wave of weakness, her body shaking, paling, slid through her, and she rubbed the part of her torso where the wood had impaled her.

She had a feeling she knew what that weakness was, and she was pissed about it. Lily and Jamie had both felt it when they'd met their true halves before cementing the bond. Becca had a feeling Nadie felt it as well, though Nadie wasn't saying anything about it.

Hunter had to be her mate, her true half.

The one who would show her what it meant to be part of the supernatural world and allow her to become...something.

Yet he'd left her alone.

Well, hell, she wouldn't stand for that. She'd get on with her business and either forget him or find him on her own. There was no way she'd just sit back and swoon over a man she'd only met twice but knew she had a connection with.

She'd have to confront him on his turf and figure out what the hell he meant when he said he'd take care of her before he left. If, at that point, she couldn't see a way for things to work, she'd leave, but there was no way she'd let things go to shit without trying first.

It wasn't in her nature.

Plus her body ached as if she'd just gotten over the flu or a really bad cold. She wanted to know if she could become something...more. Hunter seemed to be the key to that, and she'd be damned if she'd lose the promise of a future because she didn't talk to him.

Becca blinked at her reflection again then walked out of the bathroom. There was no use beating herself up now when she had a job to do, a job she might have enjoyed at one time. She knew now, though, she needed to move on eventually.

She nodded at Dante, who raised a pierced brow, but she didn't tell him the spider had won this round.

Dante owned and operated Dante's Circle, one of the oldest bars in town, but because of the various attacks on her and her friends, the place had been renovated a few times in the past year. The dark wood paneling had chips and dents in it from when the wind had rocked through the place during the last djinn-made storm, but it had been cleaned and polished to look almost new in spite of that. Pictures and other memories littered the walls, each in new or repaired frames.

Dante had wanted a place that would remind people of who they were and where they came from—at least if they knew the dragon personally. Or as personally as anyone could get to Dante. Despite having to clean up the mess of an evil that had threatened them, he'd succeeded.

It was something that Becca wanted to do in her own bar

when she had one. She hadn't known it would be her goal when she'd first walked in as an eighteen-year-old needing a place to work—and sleep—but Dante had taken her under his wing, and she'd blossomed.

It had been over twelve years since she'd stepped foot in the place, and she was ready to move on. She'd finished high school through online courses, and despite the fact that she struggled in school, she was almost done with her masters in business management.

She'd scrimped and saved and was ready to finish school and start her own life.

She knew Dante would have given her the money to start on her own—he was like that—but she wanted—no, *needed*—to do it on her own.

"Becca? You okay?" Nadie asked as she walked up to her at the bar. Petite and blonde, Becca always thought her friend looked like a fairy. Considering that fairies were probably real, Becca wouldn't be surprised if that was actually the case.

"I'm fine, just getting ready to finish my shift," she replied. The place was dying down since it was almost ten on a weeknight, and there was no game tonight. Luckily Becca didn't have to close down, so she could leave soon.

Nadie smiled then grimaced as her face paled. Becca reached out to catch her friend as she fell, but Dante was faster. She had no idea how he got over the bar so quickly, but before Becca could blink, Dante had Nadie wrapped in his arms, the concern on his face terrifying.

"Let me go," Nadie whispered, unmistakable hurt in her tone. "I'm fine, Dante."

He rubbed her shoulder slightly then nodded. His own face paled slightly as the color seeped back into Nadie's.

"What happened?" Becca asked as she cupped Nadie's cheek. Nadie, like the rest of the women she called family, was one of her best friends. There was no way she'd let Nadie go without an explanation.

Not again.

"Just a little lightheaded," Nadie said, her voice holding no room for questions.

Screw that.

"You're lying. What's wrong?" Becca tried to pull her friend closer, but Nadie pulled right back.

"I just didn't eat enough to day. I'm fine. In fact, I feel better now. I should just head home."

"Nadie..."

"Becca, stop. I'm fine."

"I'll drive you home," Dante said, his voice holding no room for argument.

Nadie rolled her shoulders then turned from Becca to face Dante. "Don't bother. I'll just drive myself. I live only a couple blocks away, something you know. I'll be fine," she repeated.

Dante furrowed his brows and looked as if he were about to cup her cheek then stopped himself. Damn, these two were going to kill her with their unsettled issues.

Though in reality, she wasn't one to talk.

"Fine, if that's what you want," Dante said then walked away without another word.

Nadie seemed to struggle for composure then gave Becca a hug. "I'll see you tomorrow. Stay safe."

Becca watched as her friend left the bar, leaving an upset dragon in her wake. Nadie didn't normally come by on a weeknight since she would have to work in the morning, there had to be something more to her being there but Becca wasn't sure she wanted to know. Thank the gods Dante liked her because she was not in the mood to figure out how to tame him.

If there even was a way.

Someone called out to her, and she got back to work. She made it thirty minutes before cutting herself on a broken glass.

"Fuck."

"What the hell did you do this time?" Dante asked as he pulled out the daily-used first-aid kit.

"Just cut my finger," she answered as she put her finger under a stream of water. "It's not deep."

"So no stitches?" He pulled her to the back of the bar and sat her on a stool before taking a look at the cut. He was getting too good at taking care of her.

"Nope. At least I hope not. I'm not in the mood for another hospital visit."

"Sorry I'm not a healing dragon, or I'd just take care of all your injuries with ease."

She cocked her head. "There are such things as healing dragons?"

He just lifted his lip in a smile. "Sure."

Becca rolled her eyes. "You're never gonna show me what you look like, are you?"

He raised a pierced brow. "Maybe one day."

She let him put a Band-Aid on her finger, and then they got back to work. She was just about to finish her last table when she dropped the check. As she reached down to pick it up, the hard pinch on her ass surprised her.

"What the fuck?" she yelled as she turned to face the sleazy man in a business suit and loosened tie.

"Just feeling the goods. If you didn't want to be touched, you shouldn't have flaunted that sweet ass or those fuckable tits in front of me."

Becca blinked, surprised by his crude words. Sure, she'd dealt with pricks before, but they weren't usually so blatant after they got caught.

"Excuse me?"

"Why don't you come sit on my lap, and I'll show you what I mean." He gripped his crotch, and Becca resisted the urge to vomit.

She flashed back to the time when another man had been over her and Hunter had saved her.

She wasn't in that position now though, and she'd be damned if she'd let the man get away with it.

"Get out of here. Now."

"You don't own this place, bitch."

"No, but I do," Dante growled from behind her. "Want me

to take care of this, Becs?"

She shook her head. "No. I can deal with it."

"Oh yeah, baby? You're gonna deal with it?" He rubbed his cock through his pants, and Becca swallowed down the bile that rose in her throat.

Seriously? This dude had to be out of his mind.

He reached out again, and she punched the bastard in the nose. Blood spurted, and he screamed like the pussy he was.

"You bitch! I'm gonna sue you!"

"No, you aren't," she said calmly. "You're gonna walk out of here and get in a cab and never come back. If you try to sue, I'll charge you with harassment and assault."

Dante crossed his large forearms across his chest and glared. "I don't see why you don't charge him now."

"Then I'd have to see him again. Get out."

He stumbled out the door, and Becca's shoulders sank. "Gods, I'm tired."

"Go home, Becs. I'll clean your section." Dante brought her into a hug that reminded her she had friends she could lean on if needed.

"Thanks. I'm whipped, and I still have to finish that paper tonight."

"Jason coming over to help with that?" Dante asked, his voice oddly emotionless.

Becca frowned. "No, I don't think so. It's not like it's an exam, and why are you looking like that? It's not like Jason and I ever dated."

Plus the dude was creepy to be alone with for too long, but she wasn't about to tell Dante that. The last thing she needed was her study partner roasted on a spit as her dragon friend smiled with glee.

"Be careful. Just because your wolf is back in his Pack dealing with his disappearance doesn't mean he won't kill a man for touching what's his."

That brought her hackles up. "Excuse me? You've got to be kidding me. I'm no man's property. Hunter isn't here, and since he hasn't even spoken to me in a month, I'll refrain from thinking the wolf has any dibs on me."

"Becca, some things are done to keep those we care about safe, not because we necessarily want to do them."

Becca frowned, thinking Dante wasn't talking about just her and Hunter now.

"I don't care right now. I'm going home and writing then going to bed. It's been a little too much for me today."

Okay sure, she'd only had to deal with a couple drunks, cutting her hand, and the spider from hell, but she was just too tired to deal with it right now.

Dante nodded then walked to the back of the bar. "I'll take care of that wee little spider for you too."

She flipped him off then went to get her things. Maybe her life was slowly changing, but at least she had her friends to remind her of what she had. Now she just had to think about what she wanted and whether that included the wolf with yellow eyes who haunted her dreams.

Chapter Three

Hunter stood in front of Dante's Circle, the sunset beating down on him. He narrowed his eyes, the brown contacts he wore irritating them. He hated wearing the damn things, but yellow eyes seemed to scare the humans. He hadn't worn them the last time he'd been here, but he'd forgotten.

After spending four years battling demons and doing things that would haunt his nightmares for years to come, putting a thin film over his eyes to keep from scaring the little humans hadn't occurred to him.

People milled around in the early evening sun, talking and going about their day. Most of them were humans so they didn't realize they were venturing around a walking shadow of death. A pixie passed him and froze, her eyes widening. She blinked then scurried off, as if too afraid of what he *could* do rather than remembering that, to most predators, prey running away only egged them on.

Hunter wasn't one of those predators though. Despite his name, he didn't feel the need to hunt after prey when the one he truly wanted was within the walls in front of him. It had been a month since he'd seen Becca. A month since she'd lain in his arms, her body pale, healing.

He could still remember the howls echoing off the walls. It hadn't been until later that he'd realized those howls of anguish had been his own. Though he hadn't known much about Becca—still didn't—the wolf within him knew everything he needed to know.

Becca Quinn would be his mate—*was* his mate.

Now he just had to convince her of that.

Leaving for a month to let each other heal and work his way through the labyrinth of lies and betrayals within the Pack might not have been the best idea in retrospect. From what he knew of females, he was pretty sure leaving without any form of communication wasn't the smartest thing.

He'd have to court Becca—something he had *no* idea how it worked or what it entailed. Maybe Ambrose and Balin would help him. Even in hell, the angel and demon had known how to make Jamie smile. Hunter was pretty sure Ambrose had messed something up before they'd gone to hell in the first place. Hunter took that to mean that if the eons-old warrior angel could make mistakes and come out of it okay, surely he could.

Hopefully.

Hunter was the Beta of the Nocturne Pack, yet right at this moment, he didn't know if he had the strength to face her. He'd never had a mate before, let alone a human one—or whatever Becca was. He wasn't exactly sure, and the triad hadn't exactly been forthcoming with details.

Most wolves within his Pack mated other wolves. That was just the way of things. Wolves had one true mate— sometimes two if they were in a triad. That was it. Sure they could mate others and have children, but it wouldn't be a true mating. All other supernaturals had the same idea of true bliss.

Finding one's true half was a blessing.

A rare one.

The moment he'd stepped into that alley and had seen the red-haired goddess, he'd known she was the one for him. It had hit him like a freight train. Where most men would have thought it was crazy, Hunter had welcomed it.

He'd known she was his.

Now he just had to figure out what to do about it.

His Pack wanted him to mate—at least the ones who wanted him alive anyway. He had a true mate, but she wasn't part of the Pack. Hunter knew this would be an issue, but he really didn't care. All he wanted was the sweet-scented woman who drugged him like an elixir with her presence.

A human bumped into him and gave him a dirty look, presumably for standing in the middle of the sidewalk. He didn't blame the human for being annoyed, so he blinked at him rather than growling. The human's eyes widened, and fear seeped from him before he took off at a brisk pace in the other direction.

"Scaring people again?" Balin asked as he walked toward him from the parking lot.

Hunter shrugged but nodded toward the demon who had become his friend. "I didn't growl or bite him. I thought I was doing well."

Balin shook his head and chuckled. "You were. I don't really get it up here either." Up here being the human realm rather than the hell realm that Balin had lived in for three hundred years.

Though Hunter's own Pack was dark, gritty, and slightly demented, he still preferred it to hell.

Balin gave him an odd look then shook his head again. "We haven't seen you in a while. Did you get things taken care of?"

Hunter thought back to the looks of pity and fear within his Pack. "Not fully, but I've been away long enough."

"You're not going to tell me what you needed to do, are you?"

"I can't." It was true. Though Balin had helped save Hunter's life, he wasn't Pack. Some secrets needed to remain within the confines of their own species—something the demon should understand.

"You're here for Becca, aren't you?" Balin crossed his large arms over his chest and glared.

Not that Hunter knew exactly why the demon happened to be glaring, but it didn't sit easy with him. Hunter's hackles rose, but he toned them down. It was good that Becca had people to take care of her—even if the warnings were misplaced.

"Yes. She's mine," he answered simply.

Balin narrowed his eyes. "Remember that these women

are not like those you know." The demon looked around at the humans who were oblivious to the rising tension. "Let's go inside. We can talk a little more freely there."

"You'd stand in the way of a bond?"

Balin shook his head and led them to the front door. "No, but I will stand before her to ensure it's what she wants. You left her high and dry and confused as hell a month ago. Don't think you can just prowl in and think everything will be okay."

Hunter frowned. "I know I will have to court her. I plan to ask you and your mates for help."

Balin blinked, his hand on the door. "You're going to ask for help? I thought you were an Alpha wolf."

"I'm the Beta of my Pack, but I'm a dominant. That doesn't mean I don't know how to ask for help when it's necessary. Becca isn't of my Pack, and I want her to remain safe. Bringing her into my Pack right now would be dangerous without all the facts, and I don't plan on forcing her to be with me."

Balin snorted then opened the door, leading them into the bar. "You're saying all the right things, but I have a feeling you'll act all wolf and think she should bend for you."

Hunter clenched his fists. "I'm not as enlightened as some. Fate made her for me, and the course has been set. I will not break from that."

The sweet scent of mate and woman filled his nose, and he turned to see the goddess of his dreams. She'd put her curly red hair in a tangle on the top of her head so little ringlets fell down her neck. Those pieces seemed to beg for his touch, and he had to remember not to reach out to her just yet. Her long neck would be perfect for his tongue, as would her ample breasts. There were more than a handful, and he wanted to know the color of her nipples.

Would they be a dusky rose or a dark red when he licked and sucked them so they became pointed peaks? Her waist was a tiny thing that flared out to hips that would be perfect for his hands as he gripped her, pummeling into her heat from behind.

Her ass was perfect, not those small ones that women seemed to love, but with enough meat on her to make his mouth water. He couldn't wait to see her naked and wondered if those freckles that dotted her nose were anywhere else. He had a feeling he'd love licking each and every one, learning her curves and her taste.

Those jade green eyes bored holes into him as they lit fire. She tapped her foot, then raised her chin. It seemed his mate wasn't happy to see him. He'd known this would be the case, though the wolf within him seemed disappointed she didn't immediately rush into his arms and declare her undying love and need.

No worries. That would come.

He ignored the other patrons as he strolled toward her. He knew he moved more like an animal than man, but he didn't care. Becca would have to learn he was a wolf, not the man she might have dreamed of.

Fate wouldn't give him a mate who couldn't accept the animal within him.

It had already been cruel enough.

He stood in front of her, their bodies a whisper apart. Her scent enraptured him, holding him close.

She tilted her head and blinked at him. "You're back."

Hell, her voice had a soft, husky quality that went straight to his balls. His cock strained at the zipper of his jeans, and his body broke out in a sweat. He didn't usually wear a shirt unless, like now, he was in public because his body was naturally overheated and the wolf made his skin feel tight, itchy, and now he was regretting putting the damn thing on. The white button-down he had on now felt confining. He'd rolled up the sleeves so his forearms could breathe, the dark tan of his skin looking deeper against the white of his shirt, yet it didn't help.

This woman made him want more and everything, yet he didn't even know her.

That would change.

Soon.

"I'm back," he said, his voice more of a growl than the calm tone he'd meant to use. "I'll always come back for you, my Becca."

She rolled her eyes then moved to the side, as if trying to get around him. Well, there would be none of that. He moved with her, and she stopped, her chin rising.

"Move, Hunter. I have work to do."

Hunter blinked and looked around the room. People stared at him as though he'd grown a second head—or had shifted into his wolf. Ambrose, Balin, and Jamie sat at the corner table with small smiles on their faces. Jamie even gave him a little finger wave, though Ambrose pulled her hand back to him then kissed her palm.

"I'll help you then." His only plan at this point was to ensure Becca's safety and bring her into his life. He'd had to leave her for too long as it was because of his Pack and his own darkness. He'd stay by her side now no matter what—even if it meant serving beer and hot wings to men who shouldn't be looking at his mate in that fashion.

On second thought, he'd enjoy working with Becca. Not only could he watch the way she moved, but now he could kill anyone who dared look at her.

His wolf growled in agreement.

Good. That was settled.

"Uh, Hunter, you're growling," Becca whispered as she put her hand on his chest.

He froze, his body going on alert at that slight touch.

"Do you not like when I do that?" It would bother him if she didn't like his wolf, but he'd show her that she had nothing to fear.

She turned her head, her green eyes narrowing. "I don't know what I feel about it, but that's not the point. Stop doing it in public please. I don't want you to get in trouble," she whispered.

Hunter leaned down as if to hear her better, though his senses were just fine to hear her from across the room.

"I'm sorry," he whispered back. "I'll help you today."

She shook her head. "No, I don't need you to."

Hurt, he pulled back. It wasn't about *need*. He wanted to help her to show he'd always be by her side like a good mate. Did she not understand that?

"I don't know why you're here, or why you stayed away for so long. I know we have things to talk about, and I'm not one of those girls to shun you because we can't communicate. I really don't know what's going on, but right now, you need to go sit with Jamie and her men while I finish my shift."

"You're not telling me to go?" Hell, he sounded like a whiny teen from some angst-filled TV show rather than the Beta of the Nocturne Pack.

"I'm telling you to do what you want, like you've been doing, but if you want to talk to me, go sit with Jamie and her men."

He nodded then risked her ire by tracing her cheek with his finger. She shuddered, and he inhaled her sweet scent, which held a hint of arousal.

Good.

Her left her standing frozen and walked to the back corner where Jamie, Ambrose, and Balin sat, smirks on their faces.

"Smooth," Balin said then took a sip of his beer. "You sure know how to make the ladies swoon. Fuck!" He rubbed his side where Jamie had elbowed him, and Hunter snorted.

He sat down at the round table and took in his surroundings. He'd been too distracted by Becca to notice the bar, other than the people who could prove to be threats. The dragon hadn't changed much in his bar since the last time Hunter had been there, but he'd at least cleaned up the debris from the fight.

His hands fisted as he remembered the pale form of his mate in his arms as she'd shuddered, taking what he'd thought to be her last breath.

"Hunter?" Jamie asked. "She's fine. You don't have to

growl."

He blinked away the memories and turned to Jamie. Like the rest of Becca's friends, she was pleasing to the eye. Her brown hair and brown eyes might have seemed boring to some, but he knew the two men on either side of her thought she was the sexiest thing in the world.

"Sorry," he grumbled.

"Four years is a long time to not have to hide your abilities," Ambrose said quietly. "It's only been a few weeks since you've been back. You're allowed to not be who you once were."

That was an understatement.

"I've always been a wolf," Hunter said, his voice barely above a whisper. "I've never been *normal*. Will she accept that?"

He didn't have to state who *she* was. It was blatantly obvious.

Jamie smiled. "I don't think what you are will be a barrier. It's *who* you are and what you do that matters. As long as you explain your absence and have a damn good reason for it, I'm sure you'll come to an understanding."

Coming out of the nightmares and trying to piece together his Pack seemed like decent reasons. He just hoped Becca agreed.

"So, you want to tell us what you've been up to?" Jamie asked.

Hunter shrugged. "What I said I'd be doing when I left. I needed to take care of my Pack before I could bring in my mate."

Balin raised a brow. "And did you get everything taken care of?"

Hunter thought back to the council members and his aging Alpha but only shook his head. "Almost."

Jamie narrowed her eyes. "You better not hurt our Becca. I might be small, but I pack a mighty punch."

Hunter remembered the magic running through her veins and held himself back from bowing at her feet and baring his neck. She was a powerful djinn while he was only a lowly wolf in comparison.

"Don't forget Faith, dear," Ambrose said with a smile.

Who knew the warrior angel could smile so warmly?

"Wait. Faith?" he asked, genuinely confused. Yes, the woman he'd met seemed a bit abrasive, but he'd thought it had just been the tension of the brewing war at the time.

Balin shuddered dramatically and pulled Jamie to his side. "Let's just say if you bother Becca in any way, Faith will be there to make sure you never do it again."

"I'll keep that in mind." Really though, what could Faith do?

"I see that look, Hunter," Ambrose said, a smile in his voice. "Don't underestimate any of the lightning-struck. They were strong before the strike and are even stronger now."

Jamie beamed at him then pulled the angel closer to her and their demon. "You are *so* getting lucky tonight," she whispered.

Jealousy ate him at the words that were meant for just the three of them. He turned to watch Becca move. Though she usually moved with the grace of a dancer, sometimes she'd trip over thin air and curse under her breath. He loved the way she blushed when she tripped. He had to hold himself back a few times to keep from pulling her into his arms to make sure she was all right.

Becca just seemed a bit clumsy, but he was okay with that. If anyone made fun of her for it, he'd rip their throats out. There were perks to being the Beta of the Nocturne Pack.

He sat and listened to the triad talk about their life together and how they were working things out. Apparently in the human realm, outside the confines of a Pack or Pride, ménages were taboo. He'd known this, of course, but he'd never seen the ramifications. Some people shunned Jamie for what fate had decided for her, but she took it in stride. She seemed much happier than the small wallflower he'd met in their cell within the demon games.

He remembered looking at her and thinking, for just a moment, it would be hell to kill her...then she'd spoken. She'd been stronger than he'd thought, and he'd known he had to protect her even if she wasn't his protect.

He'd fought by her side within the games and watched as she'd taken down a full demon on her own.

Now she was in a relationship and bond that was stronger than most bonds out there. The true-half mating bond could withstand even the darkest of powers, and Hunter was glad Jamie had that.

He just needed to make sure he and Becca had the same chance. He'd never courted anyone before, let alone a human.

It would be tricky to figure out the best way of strategizing. He figured throwing her over his shoulder and taking her to his den would be out of the question.

Too bad.

Hunter watched Becca move some more. Her long legs were sexy as hell in little shorts showcasing her ass. He narrowed his eyes at a man who couldn't seem to pull his gaze from Becca's body. His wolf rose to the surface, and he let a small growl out.

The man turned to him with wide eyes and lowered his gaze. Though humans couldn't tell he was a wolf, they would instinctively know not to fuck with him...or his mate.

"Hunter, man, stop terrorizing the humans," Balin said under his breath.

Hunter turned to the demon. "The man should learn his place. He has no right to stare at Becca like that." He clenched his fists, his claws ready to fight for what was his.

"She works at a bar," Balin explained. "This stuff happens, but she can take care of herself."

"Plus Dante would kick the ass of anyone who bothered her."

At the name of the dragon, Hunter shut his eyes, fighting for control. He didn't say anything to the triad...couldn't. He didn't know what sort of relationship existed between Dante and Becca, but he knew he couldn't take down a dragon no matter how strong he was.

The dragon would have to back down on his own.

There was no room in his and Becca's relationship for a third.

Their mating wasn't like that.

"Hunter, you know Dante and Becca aren't together, right?"

He looked at Jamie, who bit her lip.

"They're just friends. Almost like brother and sister. I promise."

A small amount of relief slid through him, but until he heard those words from Becca, he wouldn't be able to relax. This whole fate thing was seriously making him crazy. Yes, he was slightly manic from his time in hell, but fate was worse. He'd taken one look at Becca and known she was his. It didn't matter if there had been no feelings before that moment because the bond would be set.

He'd just have to learn about her and she him. That was the problem with mating a true half. Where others could mate when they wanted and take their time, the mating urge that came from meeting that one person who was meant for them urged them to move faster than they would normally.

Now he was working backward—learning and courting the person he *knew* he'd spend the rest of his life with.

Becca walked over to him with a slight smile on her face. He breathed in her sweet scent, and his wolf relaxed at her presence, even though the mating urge rode him harder.

"I'm done with my shift now," she said as she came to his side. "What did you want?"

He blinked, caught by her beauty. "I'll walk you home, and we can talk."

Yes, talking. Women liked that, right?

She cocked her head and frowned. "Just talking? Because I don't know you."

He nodded and tamped down the hurt at her words. He knew they didn't know each other past that bond that wanted to form, but he would change that.

Then he'd bring her to his Pack.

Soon he found himself saying goodbye to the triad and glaring at the dragon who stood silently in the doorway. He'd have to deal with Dante later.

"Did you drive here?" Becca asked, looking around the parking lot.

"My bike is over there." He gestured to the black Harley and smiled.

She froze then looked up at him. "I usually walk or take the bus since I don't have a car."

He frowned. He didn't like the idea that she would be near strangers and in danger. "Why don't you need a car? I thought all humans did."

She shrugged. "I'm saving for my...for the future, so I just walk. It's not that far."

"You can ride behind me home. I don't want you alone."

She narrowed her gaze. "We need to get one thing straight, okay? Just because you think I'm your mate and we have this...this connection or whatever, doesn't give you the right to tell me what to do. I've been fine for over a decade alone, and I don't need you telling me what to do."

His wolf urged him to bring her into his arms and never let go, but he rebelled. "I'm not telling you what to do."

She blinked.

"Okay, fine. I tried to tell you what to do. From now on, I'll try to ask. Remember though, I'm a wolf, so it's hard to turn off those tendencies." For Becca though, he'd do anything.

They stood in the darkened parking lot alone but for the breeze. His cock strained at his jeans as she moved closer.

"I don't understand any of this, Hunter."

He nodded and took a risk, framing her face with his hands. She didn't pull away, and he took it as a good sign. "I know. I'm trying to understand it all as well."

"Why did you stay away so long? If what my friends are saying is true and we're...we're true halves, why did you leave?"

He would tell her everything soon, leaving no secret

behind, but right now, he could only say the words that meant the most.

"I wasn't worth it before. I needed to make myself worth you."

She sucked on her lip then nodded. "That doesn't tell me enough, but I know you're trying. I don't know what I want Hunter. I need choices."

Fate hadn't given them a choice, and he wouldn't argue with what could be good for him, but he just nodded.

"I'll do whatever you want. For always."

"One step at a time, Hunter. I want to know who you are and why I feel this warmth within me every time you're near. I didn't grow up with any of this. I need time."

He nodded then lowered his head, letting his lips rest gently on hers. She gasped, and he licked the seam of her mouth. She opened for him softly, her breath coming in short pants. He kissed her with a care he didn't know he possessed.

He was a wolf, an animal, not someone who was used to gentleness, but for Becca, he'd be anything she needed.

He drowned in her sweet taste, relishing her submission. Finally, he pulled back, his wolf howling in pleasure. Her eyes had darkened, and her hard nipples brushed against his shirt.

"One step at a time, Becca. Anything you need."

She smiled at him, and he knew he'd broken through that first step.

Now he just needed to show her he could be hers.

And show the Pack that she was safe.

Easier said than done.

Chapter Four

Dante Bell watched his best friend walk out the door with the wolf that would be her mate. It wasn't that he wanted Becca for himself, no, that was as far from the truth as anything. Sadly, jealousy ate at him because this fiery little friend, who couldn't seem to stand in place without knocking something over, was well on her way to finding happiness.

Though he knew the two of them had more to deal with in their future than pretty words and heated looks, he was happy for them.

He was just fucking jealous.

It wasn't as if he didn't know who his true half—or halves as it were—was. He'd known their identity for years but hadn't been able to do anything about it because there was always something in the way. Now he was starting to sound like that old fool Ambrose—something he sure as hell didn't want to be.

When the gods had decided his human friends needed a jolt, he'd watched as they'd been struck by lightning and their lives changed forever. He'd been forced to stand by and do his best to protect them, though he hadn't known who he was fighting. He *still* didn't know who he was fighting, or whether, frankly, there was something to fight. He'd stand by his friends and their mates as they found them and protect them from whatever came—even from each other.

Now he was, again, on the sidelines, waiting and praying that it would all come together so he could claim the two who'd haunted his dreams as his own.

As it was, Nadie was in pain because he couldn't act on what he knew they both needed—*craved*. He couldn't complete the bond, though, because it wouldn't be enough, not without their third.

And it was fucking hard to complete the mating if he didn't know where their third was.

So now, because of the way the lighting worked, he was forced to watch Nadie's energy and strength drain away because he couldn't bond with her. If the girls hadn't been struck by lightning in the first place, Nadie wouldn't be in pain. Sure, she'd have remained human for the rest of her life, but he'd have used their true half mating bond to make her as immortal as he. Now he had to stand by and watch her in pain because they didn't have their third...because he'd let their third walk away to go on their own journey. Of course he'd done all he could to find their third and take away Nadie's pain, but there was only so much he could do.

He took her pain deep inside his body when he could, leaving his body weakened. For some reason, whenever he took the pain from her, it magnified within him tenfold. Though she sometimes left him feeling just a bit stronger, afterward, he was forced to curl up in a ball and regain his strength. He was a fucking dragon, but there was nothing he could do for the pain and weakness.

There was also no way he'd force Nadie to deal with that—or even a small piece of that—on her own.

So now, because he couldn't do anything to protect her other than trying to help where he could, he was creating a divide between the two of them.

He knew they had only so much more time. Soon that divide would be too great for either of them to conquer.

He just hoped it wouldn't be too late.

****

"So how was it?"

Becca rolled her eyes at Faith's words since she knew her friend couldn't see her over the phone. She wouldn't have been in the mood to deal with her friend's attitude if the other woman could see her.

"How was what?" she asked.

"The kiss! Damn, Becca, stop stringing me along. I saw how hot that wolf boy was. Did you see the way he smoldered? Yes, smoldered. Who knew that happened outside of movies or books? Hell, if you don't want him, I'll take him for a ride."

"Back off, Faith. He's not for you," Becca snapped.

Faith cackled over the line. Cackled. She knew her friend, like the rest of the girls, would one day turn into another supernatural creature, and Becca was pretty sure Faith would be a witch, considering she already had the laugh down.

"Touchy, aren't we?" Faith teased. "So I guess the dude can kiss. Good for him. I hope you didn't sleep with him right away though."

"Fuck off, Faith."

"You're making me cranky over here, but I love you. Plus, if you'd slept with him, we'd all be hearing about your new powers. I can't wait to see what you turn into."

Becca wasn't sure she *wanted* to know and told Faith as much.

"Becs, you're in pain, and it's because you found Hunter and aren't mated. We've seen Jamie and Lily go through this, and we're *watching* Nadie go through it."

"I know that, hon. I know that the gods and fate and whatever want me and Hunter together, but I don't like not having a choice."

"I know what you mean. I see Lily and Jamie happy and loopy in love, but that doesn't mean it will be the same for us."

Becca rolled her eyes. "Thanks for that confidence."

"Anything you need, babe."

"You suck."

"No, not at the moment. I've been single for too long."

Becca chuckled and gagged into the phone. "I totally

don't need to know that."

"What? You started it."

"You're a dork, but I love you anyway. Really, though, I don't know what to do."

Faith sighed. "Do what you want, Becs, but know that sometimes you just have to work with what fate deals you. Don't run away from something that could be good because you're fighting the system."

"I'm going to remind you of this conversation when you find your mate."

Her friend snorted. "Gods, that's gonna suck. Everyone is going to come at me with my own words."

"Hurts, don't it?"

"Shut it, *chica*. Really, though, take it slow with Hunter and find out who he is beyond that bond you're feeling, or will feel. If the pain is too much, sleep with him."

Becca rolled her eyes. "Really? Sleep with him? That's your advice?"

Faith snorted. "What? It's the best I can give. It'll help you feel better, and you know sex relieves stress. Plus I know you had that whole connection with him after the storm with the djinn, so you feel something. This is the twenty-first century. Have fun. Have sex. I don't know what fate will bring, but we'll figure it out. I really don't get the whole thing yet. If you don't want to screw him, at least kiss him."

"So kissing is okay?"

"With the way he kisses apparently, I'd say he's more than okay."

"That's not what I mean, and you know it." Hell, sometimes Faith got on something and never let it go, like a dog with a bone.

"Just go with it, Becca. He needs to atone for leaving you for a month, but considering where he'd been for the four years prior, I'm sure he has a ready excuse."

Becca rolled her eyes. "You're sounding like you don't believe in any excuses."

"Of course not. He probably did that alpha-caveman thing where he wanted to protect you without actually saying *why*. You know, like we can't handle the big words or something."

"Stop man-hating, hon. We'll see what happens, as he should be here for dinner."

"Ooooh, a date?"

"Sure, call it what you will. First, though, I have a study session with Jason."

"Seriously? Aren't you done with that class with that freak yet?"

"He's not a freak. He's just...creepy." That seemed like the best word for the man who constantly asked her out, even though she constantly turned him down.

"I don't like the fact that he's spending so much time with you."

"He helps me study, Faith. He's never made a move beyond asking me out and always lets the subject go as soon as I tell him no. We work well together beyond that, and he's really helping me ace this class."

Her friend snorted. "You're brilliant without him, but if you want to study with him, fine. Just remember to punch him like you did with that dude from the bar if he crosses the line. Oh, and make sure he's out of the house before Hunter shows up. The last thing you need is a wolf who's pissed some douche is encroaching on his territory."

"It's not like that with Jason, so Hunter shouldn't have a problem with it. How do you know so much about wolves and alpha men by the way?"

"Uh, no reason," Faith hedged.

"Faith, spill."

"Fine. I've been reading some of Jamie's romance novels."

Becca held back a laugh but rolled her eyes. "You know those aren't real, right? They don't actually tell you what you need to know about the supernatural."

"Maybe they don't tell me exactly how Hunter is as a wolf, but it helps with the whole alpha-male thing. He's not going to want another man sniffing around what's his."

At the mental image of Hunter sniffing like a dog, Becca knew it was time to call it quits.

"Okay, you need to back away from the romance novels if you think they're real life."

"It's not that. Oh, shut it. You don't understand. Just make sure Jason is out of the place and spray it down with air freshener or something. You don't want a pissed-off wolf on your hands. Wait, maybe not air freshener. Won't that hurt Hunter's senses? There really has to be a Paranormal for Dummies book out here, don't you think?"

"Whatever you say, Faith. Now I've got to go. Jason will be here any minute."

"Be safe, Becs. Please."

"I will. Love ya."

"Love ya too."

They hung up, and Becca went out to her living room to make sure she had everything ready for her study session. She wasn't like Lily with her clean piles of notepads, sticky notes, and color-coordinated highlighters, but she at least was pleasantly organized. This would, thankfully, be the last one with Jason, and Becca wasn't upset at all about that.

When Jason knocked on the door ten minutes later, she was beyond ready to get it over with. The exam was in two days, and then she'd be free.

Thank the gods.

Jason, like usual, strolled through the living room as though he owned the place. With his dark auburn hair and darker green eyes, Becca supposed he was attractive, but she'd never really seen it. Sure, he had that chiseled-face thing girls loved, but there was only one man with dark looks and a swagger who could make her swoon.

Not that she'd ever swoon in Hunter's presence.

No, not ever.

"Jamie, darling, you look as intoxicating as ever," Jason said, his voice smarmy.

Well, he might not have actually sneered, but it sure has hell sounded that way to Becca at the moment.

How the hell was she supposed to make it another two hours with the man who made her want to shower off the sleaze?

"Hey, Jason. Ready for our final study session?"

The man pouted. Pouted. *Would it be too late and rude to slam the door in his face and feign sickness?* "I don't want our time to end, baby doll."

She was going to just ignore the not-so-vague meaning of his words and plow right through it. "Well, we're almost done with school, so let's just focus on that."

Jason brightened at that. "Yes, school. Even though that's ending, Becca, that doesn't mean *we* have to end."

Dear gods, she needed an aspirin. Or a frying pan to throw at the dude. Yes, a frying pan could work. If only she had Shade's cast iron pan that he loved to use when he was cooking for *his* Lily.

"Jason, there is no *we*."

He moved toward her, and she stayed where she was. She wasn't about to back away and show that he freaked her out. She was stronger than that.

Maybe.

"Oh, Becca, darling, there could be a *we*. All you have to do is say the word, and I'll take you in my arms and never let you go. You know we're meant to be together."

Could this man be any more delusional?

He placed his hand on her shoulder, and she flinched.

"Back away, Jason. I've told you over and over that we're not a couple, that we won't ever *be* a couple. Why don't you get that?"

"Yes, why don't you get that?"

Becca froze and turned toward Hunter, who filled her doorway. His eyes narrowed, and his lips lifted in a snarl.

Oh shit, Faith had been right. This could *not* end well.

"Hunter, it's not what you think." Becca grimaced. Well, that didn't come out the right way at all.

When had her life turned into a horribly written soap opera?

Hunter's gaze never left Jason's, but he did clench his fists a bit more. Was it wrong that she found that alphaness sexy as hell? With his long brown hair brushing his shoulders and his wide shoulders and narrow hips, he looked perfect for her.

Maybe he'd taste as good as he looked.

All. Over.

She blinked, forcing her mind off his delectable body and back on the fact that Jason could possibly be staring his own death in the face.

There would be no way she could get the blood out of the carpet.

Apparently she'd been spending too much time with supernaturals if that was the first thought that occurred to her.

"Becca, can you please remove yourself from this male's grip?" Hunter asked on a growl. "I don't want you to get hurt."

Jason scoffed at that and pulled her behind him.

Stupid idiot.

Hunter growled again, and Becca moved from behind Jason. "Stop it. Both of you."

"I haven't said a thing, darling," Jason drawled.

Yep, she was gonna kill the dude. Slowly.

Becca risked a glance at Hunter's face, only to see a snarl.

Okay, maybe she'd kill Jason quickly so Hunter wouldn't have to.

"I'm not your fucking darling. You need to go, Jason. I don't need your help studying this time. In fact, I should have turned you away before."

He turned to face her, a mix of anger and disbelief on his face. "You can't be serious. You're turning me away for this overgrown ape?"

Hunter didn't react to that comment. In fact it looked as

if he were using all his strength not to come closer and take over the situation—tearing Jason limb from limb in the process.

"Go, Jason. I'm not picking him over you." Hunter growled again, and she put her hand up to silence him. "You were never in the running. You've been hitting on me for months, and I've tried to be nice because I thought we could be friends. Well, screw that. You need to go. I'm done dealing with your creepy shit."

"You'll be sorry, Becca. This isn't over. Not by a long shot. I *will* be back."

"Did you just threaten me?" Now it was Becca's turn to gape in disbelief.

"You have two seconds to leave, Jason, before I take care of this for her," Hunter warned.

Well, at least he'd tried to hold back for bit. That had to count for something, right?

"You're a bitch, you know that?" Jason didn't wait for her response. Hunter moved out of the way as if he didn't want to touch the bastard, and Becca didn't blame him, as Jason stormed out of the apartment with his bag in tow.

The man who could be her mate stalked toward her, his pace more like an animal than the man she saw, but she didn't care.

He ran his fingers over her face then down her shoulders where Jason had touched her. "You smell of him," he murmured.

"He's never touched me before, but I'll go spray myself down with something if his scent bothers you."

"No, don't. Sprays and perfumes are usually too much for my senses. I'll take care of it though."

Confused, she looked at him then froze as he ran his hands along her side then lowered his head to nuzzle her neck and shoulder with his face.

"What...what are you doing?" Not that she disliked it or anything, but it was...weird. Okay, not weird, but...different.

"Scent marking you," he answered, his deep voice

vibrating along her skin.

"Oh, okay. Do I need to move or anything?" Apparently she was okay with scent marking. Who knew?

He gave a raspy chuckle as if he weren't used to laughing. Damn whoever had sent him to hell; she'd make him laugh more. "You're fine where you are. I love the way you feel."

"Oh, well, you feel nice too."

Wow. Really, Becca? That's the best you can do?

He ran his hands up and down her sides then framed her face. "Hello."

"Hi. You're early."

He grinned. "Sorry. I couldn't stay away."

"I'm glad you're here though."

"Yes, to deal with that fool."

"No, I mean, yes. I could have taken care of him on my own."

"I don't like him."

"Hunter, you don't have to worry about him. I'm not seeing anyone."

"Including Dante?" He turned his head like a wolf rather than a man, and she started.

"Dante? Uh, no. Hell no. He's...he's Dante. He's not mine."

"Good, because you're mine."

She pulled back from his grip. "Wait. You need to hold off on those dominating and possessive words."

"Why? I want you. You want me. I can scent it."

She blushed and closed her eyes. Damn wolf. "Uh, try not to do that. Please."

"I can't help it, Becca. You smell sweet."

Oh holy hell.

"Stop it." It wasn't fair that she couldn't scent him like that. She forced herself not to look down to see the physical evidence of his arousal. That was the last thing she needed.

"It's not something to be embarrassed about. I like that you find me desirable. I feel the same way about you. After all, we're mates."

"About that... can we take this slow? I'm not going to run away and lie about what I'm feeling, but first, I want to understand it."

He gazed at her then nodded. "Whatever you need."

"Then we can date first."

"Date?"

Becca snorted. "I mean you and I can hang out, go to dinner, and do things together. Just hold off on the whole fate-thing for a bit while we get to know each other. Or, at least, let me finish school, and then we can take the whole supernatural thing into consideration."

Hunter blinked. "Does this mean we can't make love?"

Images of his very tanned and sweaty body riding hers filled her mind, and she groaned.

"I think I like where your mind just went," he said with a smile in his voice.

"Hunter, stop saying things like that. Let's just get to know one another. We can talk about...sex later."

"It wouldn't just be sex between us, Becca."

Oh, she was sure what he said was right. Damn, this was going to be harder than she thought.

"We can kiss, Hunter, but that's it. Let's just take this on its natural progression."

"The natural progression would be to mate and have me sink into your heat over and over again."

Was it possible to have an orgasm from just words spoken in a growl?

"Now you're just saying these things to tease me."

He looked serious for a moment then framed her face again. "I would never tease you beyond wanting to see your pleasure. I will take it slow because you ask this of me. Now, can I kiss you?"

Becca nodded, her tongue too heavy to speak. Hunter grinned then lowered his lips to hers. Gods, they were so soft, yet so unyielding. She couldn't wait to feel them against other parts of her body.

She moaned into his mouth and rocked against him. His jean-clad erection brushed her belly, and he moaned right back.

She pulled away, breathless. "Well, we seem to have that part down."

Hunter smiled, his teeth a stark white against the tan of his skin. He leaned closer and bit down on her lower lip then licked the sting. "Oh, I would think we'd have few things down. I'm not letting you go, Becca Quinn. You are mine."

For some reason, no matter what she'd told herself before, those words made her want to think about the future and what it would mean to have him by her side.

Holding back and not jumping headfirst into the unknown would be harder than she thought.

She stared into his brown eyes. They had a rim of yellow around his contacts.

Yes, much, much harder.

****

Nadie Morgan gripped the edge of her pedestal sink and groaned. Another wave of pain ebbed through her, and she forced back the bile that threatened to rise in her throat.

Her once lustrous blonde hair was lank and clung to her face as her body broke out in a sweat. Her violet eyes stared back at her from her reflection but didn't have the same spark they'd once had.

She was dying.

That had to be it.

Damn him.

Damn that stupid dragon.

She'd had a crush on the man since she was barely eighteen, and now the crush had transformed into something that wasn't normal. She might have fallen in love with the man he was and the dragon she knew he hid from her, but that didn't mean he loved her back.

Since the lightning had struck, she'd been forced to stand back and watch as her friends found the loves of their lives. Shade hadn't waited long to declare himself for Lily. Ambrose had been gone for a year because of his council and had fought back to be by Jamie's side. Balin had risked his life without even knowing who Jamie was before he made her his. Nadie knew Hunter would claim Becca any day now—once he knew it was safe.

Yet Dante had done nothing.

Oh, she knew that connection, that cord that could bring them together was there, but he ignored it. He stood back and watched as her once-vibrant self had faded to almost nothing.

She lashed out, and he'd taken it with nothing but a look of sorrow.

What did he have to feel sorrowful about?

He was killing her with his lack of action, and she was weak enough to take it.

Well, no more.

She slammed her hands on the sink and cursed.

She was done with waiting for a man who wouldn't have her. He might be her true half, but that didn't mean it was his decision.

She'd walk away or find another way.

Dante was hers, and she'd either have him or find another way to live.

She wouldn't wallow anymore.

She had to be stronger.

Chapter Five

Hunter wasn't sure he would be able to wait any longer for Becca to give in to their mating. It had already been two weeks since he'd come to her and told her it was time. In retrospect, telling a human—a human *woman*—that their mating had to occur right then might not have been the best thing to do.

No, she'd told him they'd have to take it slow, so that's what he was doing.

Dating her slow and steady would have been okay if he'd been human. Eating meals, watching movies, and doing other things in public was nice, but his wolf was on edge. He spent every night with her.

Watching.

Waiting.

Enjoying.

He'd do anything for her, but hell, he needed a cold shower or a quick dip in the lake after each date.

Waiting, however, was killing him.

He was a wolf, not a man, so standing back and watching her take her time and do...human things made him feel as though he was betraying his animal half. He knew that wasn't the case, but it didn't help matters that all he wanted to do in her presence was strip her down and feast on her sweet taste.

Apparently that would be moving too fast.

On four paws rather than two feet, Hunter ran through the forest, letting his wolf take over. They were on their sanctioned full moon hunt. They ran as a Pack, rather than the disillusioned men and women they were quickly becoming.

Contrary to the popular lore, their wolves didn't need to turn at the full moon and could turn when they needed as long as they had the energy. The more dominant the wolf, the faster they could change and the less recovery time they needed. Though each change hurt like a bitch due to the fact they were literally rearranging their bones and tissues, they pushed through it because it was in their nature.

Some of the more submissive wolves could change as quickly as a more dominant wolf because their power sat differently. They were the *strongest* of the submissives, something that not everyone understood.

Also unlike what was stated in the lore, they weren't vicious beasts—half man, half wolf—who walked on two legs and looked like horror movie rejects. No, they looked like wolves and were only slightly bigger than their animal counterparts. Most people couldn't even tell the difference. They ran in a wide array of natural colors and had the same colored eyes they had in human form—usually gold but for a few special members.

Those Pack members with blue eyes were usually treasured and cared for beyond measure because they were submissive, and the stronger wolves *needed* to care for them— not that all submissives had blue eyes either. Hunter held back a growl at the thought of one of the submissive wolves who hadn't been treated like the treasure she was. Leslie Masterson was the younger sister of Dorian, a council member, and she'd been treated like a pet, rather than the strong woman that hid beneath the downcast eyes.

He'd fix that.

Not only was it his job as Beta, but he also liked the girl like the little sister he never had.

Hunter leaped over a fallen tree, letting the scent of the forest wash over him. He'd missed this. Damn, he'd missed this. He could feel his Pack around him, their movements in sync as they hunted their prey—whether it be a rabbit or willing partner.

For wolves, the hunt led to violence or sex. Always. They'd either kill a rabbit, deer, or something non-human, or find another wolf to fuck hard into the ground. They killed in wolf form, mated in human form. He could sense some of the female wolves around him, their arousal filling his nostrils, but he ignored them. They wanted the freak from hell who'd been gone so long. They wanted a hard fuck from the Beta of the Pack and hope for a mating.

He had Becca and didn't need another wolf to fill her place while she took her time deciding what she wanted—though they both knew what she wanted and were only giving it time because rushing head-first into a mating as a human didn't seem like the best choice.

He wouldn't fault her for that and would wait.

Alone.

He growled at a female who got too close but kept the growl soft so he wouldn't anger her. He didn't want to piss off someone who just wanted contact, but he wasn't about to send mixed signals.

She tossed her head then ran off to find another male. When the wolf rode them hard, it didn't matter to most who they found to satisfy the need.

Liam and Alec ran on either side of him, their dominant power seeping off of them as they pushed harder. His ear twitched as the sound of a rabbit's frantic chase began. He inhaled, that tangy taste of prey hitting his wolf.

He ran harder, Liam and Alec following. He pounced on the rabbit and dug his teeth into its flesh. It died a quick death— Hunter wasn't one to let it suffer—and Hunter began his meal, his wolf happy with the hunt.

Liam and Alec each found a rabbit of their own, and they feasted until their bellies were partially full and the moon trickled over their fur. He hadn't been on a hunt in over four years. He could have gone when he got back, but he'd been more animal than man and had needed space.

In retrospect that might have been the wrong decision

because it kept him from his Becca for too long.

He knew he was paying for that now. Maybe not consciously, but he had a feeling it was on her mind.

He shook off his slight doubt and howled to the moon. Liam and Alec joined him, their own howls melding into a perfect harmony. Others howled as they found their conquests, their hunts ending.

He trotted past other wolves eating their dinners in animal form, and they lowered their eyes, their power not as dominant as his. Grunts and slaps reached his ears, and his wolf perked up at the smell of sex in the air. Pack members in human form fucked in corners and shadows, their partners in ecstasy. Some were with their mates, others with random men or women. Most wolves were bisexual, considering there weren't that many women, and sex was a natural process, not something to be looked down on. Hunter himself had been with men, but preferred women.

Well, woman, now, thinking of Becca.

The woman who, as a wolf, had shown her eagerness to him currently knelt on all fours as Dorian plowed into from behind. The other male wolf didn't much mind that the woman wasn't getting off but rather faking the noises and movements so Dorian could enjoy himself. The man was a sadist in every meaning of the word, and Hunter was just glad he didn't have to see all of what went on behind his closed doors.

As the three of them—he, Liam and Alec—passed, Dorian lifted a lip and snarled, his grip tightening on the woman, Sandra. She rolled her eyes but otherwise looked as though she was fine.

Hunter wasn't in the mood to get in a fight with the man, but he'd protect Sandra if she needed it. Instead, he, Liam, and Alec made their way back to his home then shifted back, the tearing of tendons and breaking of bones a sweet pain. He shifted faster than the other two, but not by much. There was a reason Liam and Alec were council members.

Hunter threw on some jeans but didn't bother with a

shirt. Though he'd let his wolf play, his skin was still too itchy to deal with the fabric.

"Council meeting in five minutes," Liam called from the other room.

"Didn't we just have one?" Alec said with a grunt.

"No, that was the Beta ceremony," Liam explained as Hunter walked in the living room.

The two men were sitting on Hunter's couch in jeans but hadn't put on shirts either. He'd have to make sure they dressed for when Becca came to live with him. There was no way he'd let the two of them walk around so freely in front of her. It was true that the Pack didn't bother with modesty unless they were in the den center or near were the pups played, but he didn't think Becca would think the same way.

Plus he wanted to keep her for himself.

His wolf nudged at his skin again, and he held back a growl.

Waiting for her was taking too long. He'd have to go to her home again and ask for another...date, as she put it.

"What's got you looking like you're ready to tear out someone's throat?" Liam asked.

"Nothing." He hadn't mentioned Becca to them yet for some reason, and he didn't want to deal with the matter now. She would be there soon enough.

"You're lying, but I'll let you pass on that for now," Alec said. "Now we need to leave, or we'll be late for the council meeting."

"The council shouldn't have the power to call the Alpha and Beta in whenever they want," Hunter grumbled as they made their way to the council chambers, away from their homes.

Liam held up both hands in mock surrender. "Josiah agreed to it, so we're having the meeting. Don't get on my ass for it."

"I want nothing to do with your ass, Liam," Hunter said. "I'm just pissed that on the night of our hunt I have to go sit and listen to the other three members of the council bitch and moan about something that has nothing to do with them."

Alec nodded solemnly. "I agree. Why do you think Liam and I stay on the council? Without us, who knows what the other three would do?"

Hunter held back a shudder at that and reached out to squeeze Alec's shoulder, ignoring the odd look on Liam's face. They'd deal with the latter later. "I know I don't say it enough, but thank you for being here. Thank you for taking care of Samuel when I could not."

That familiar stab of pain echoed through him at the mention of his brother's name, but he put that away. He didn't want to think about the boy who'd been too young to lead by Josiah's side and had lost his life because of it.

"We weren't enough," Alec whispered.

Liam growled. "No, but we'll find out who did it—and who sent you to hell."

Hunter started, looking at the wolf he called friend. Though they'd all tiptoed around the fact that a member of the Pack had betrayed him, they hadn't outright stated it. The fact that Liam and Alec were on his side almost sent him to his knees.

Hell, he wasn't alone.

Overcome with an emotion he didn't want to name, he gave the other wolf a nod then walked into the council chambers. The room was in a horseshoe shape with five seats surrounding a center where someone could stand and bare witness or counsel. There were two seats higher than those of the council members for the Alpha and Beta.

According the some of the council members, those seats were just for show, but Hunter would be damned if he'd let the council meet without him. The council was supposed to only advise, not govern.

The Pack wasn't a democracy. The Alpha held the power to rule over the Pack, and in return, their wolves would gain the power of knowing they were protected by not only Josiah, but the Beta as well.

The council, however hard they tried, would not be able to change that.

Hunter would make sure of it.

Fate and the gods had ensured it for generations before him.

Dorian, Gregory, and Alistair already sat at their places. Gregory and Alistair whispered to each other about mundane things. Silly to whisper when a wolf was around, but those two seemed to want to be human no matter the insanity of the issue.

Dorian, on the other hand, draped himself over the chair. His pants were zipped, but not buttoned. The sated look on his face only made Hunter want to claw him more because he knew Sandra was probably still wanting—something that could be dangerous for a wolf, male or female. He himself didn't have his Becca, leaving him aching just the same.

Josiah sat on his throne, a carefully blank, yet just as fierce, expression on his face. No matter what people thought, what Hunter himself had once thought, Josiah was stronger than them all. He played the soft ruler when it was needed and killed when others would not in the name of peace. His wolf could shift the fastest, and his own strength outweighed the strength of any other.

The only downfall to a strong Alpha was that they needed an even stronger Beta to balance that power.

When Hunter had been gone, Josiah had looked weakened. He might have been Beta before all this had happened, but when he'd come back, he had to prove himself all over gain. It made no sense to some, but to wolves, proving one's self never ended.

When Hunter's brother Samuel had stepped in when no other could, it hadn't been enough. As council members, Liam and Alec hadn't been able to become Beta, even if their power and level of dominance would have made it easier. Samuel might have been a dominant wolf but hadn't had the power to take care of his Pack. Nor had he known the politics enough to keep himself alive.

Liam and Alec took their seats while Hunter made his way to his.

"Wait, Hunter," Gregory drawled. "You need to stand in the middle."

His wolf clawed at him, pissed at the command in the man's tone. "Did you just order me?"

Gregory paled slightly but didn't say anything.

"We're not ordering you," Dorian said, the lie evident in his voice. "We've summoned the council to talk about the Beta. It would behoove you to stand in the center."

"Summoned?" Hunter raised a brow.

Behoove? Who knew the other wolf knew such big words.

Dorian rolled his eyes. "It's a council meeting. You know what I mean."

"Why I am I the subject?" Hunter growled, glaring at Liam and Alec.

His two *friends* shook their head, and Hunter tensed. If they didn't know the topic of the council meeting, then something was up, though with each recent council meeting, something was *always* up.

Josiah growled from his perch but didn't say anything.

Fuck, this couldn't be good.

"You need a mate," Alistair commanded.

Hunter blinked. "Excuse me?"

"By law, as Beta, you need a mate," Dorian said, a slight edge to his tone. "Because your Alpha decreed you to be Beta again, it was past time to ensure the laws are followed."

Hunter growled. "First, he's your Alpha as well."

Josiah let out a small snarl, the power leaking through and sending shivers down Hunter's back. Fuck, the man could be deadly if needed. The others in the room looked even more pained.

Good.

"Second, I didn't have mate before, so why bother forcing the agenda now?"

"You dare question the authority of the council?" Gregory

sneered.

"I'm the Beta. I'll question who the fuck I want," Hunter replied, his voice calm.

"Why should we force the issue?" Liam asked, interrupting the growing tension.

"Just because you're fuck buddies with the Beta doesn't mean he gets special treatment," Dorian sneered. "He should have had a mate before."

"Watch your tongue, wolf," Alec whispered, his voice a lethal blade.

Dorian only smiled. "I have a few wolves for you if you can't find a mate. My sister for one."

Hunter growled. The man was actually bargaining off his sister? For what?

"I already have a mate."

He saw Liam and Alec tense slightly but didn't say anything. He knew he'd hurt them by not saying something sooner, but it hadn't been time yet. Becca was still new...still *his*.

"Convenient," Alistair spat. "Where is this mate of yours, and why haven't we heard of this before?"

"I only met her when I got back from hell. You know, the place that I spent four years nearly dying in? Let's make sure we discuss that at some point soon, shall we?"

Gregory waved his question away. "We'll talk of that later. Who is this person who is suddenly your mate?"

"She's in the human realm." Technically, as wolves, they were also in the human realm, they were, in fact, hidden from prying eyes, which helped distinguish the difference.

"A human?" Dorian's lip curled, and he spat on the ground in clear disgust. "I won't be having a human coming into the Pack and diluting the bloodlines."

"She's not just my mate," Hunter growled. "She's my true half, and you have no authority over fate, me, or my mate."

Again, Liam and Alec started but didn't say anything. Hunter knew they'd have plenty to say in private, but now was not the time.

Josiah, on the other hand, broke out in a grin. "This is the best news I've heard since you came back to us, Hunter, my son." His gaze traveled around the council. "Fuck your thoughts on the bloodlines. You all have something else in your family tree. Fate has degreed Hunter a mate, and so it shall be."

"I say we celebrate this new mating and call this meeting to an end," Liam said with a smile and moved with an athletic grace to the center of the room.

"This isn't over," Dorian said.

Alec disagreed. "It's over. The Beta will have his mate, and our Pack will be stronger for it. You know true halves are rare. This should be a time of joy, not a discussion on bloodlines."

Josiah stood and left the room, his head held high. Hunter prowled out of the room, making sure his Alpha's back was safe. No matter the feeling racing through his veins, Hunter would always protect his Alpha—especially from council members who didn't get their way.

Their Alpha paused and turned back toward them. "Congratulations, boy. We need to talk soon."

"Yes. I've missed too much."

Josiah nodded then went back to his home while Liam and Alec fell in line beside Hunter.

"You'll explain?" Liam asked.

"She's human and needs time."

"You have any idea what you're going to do about her?" Alec asked.

"Find a way to bring her into the Pack and keep her safe," Hunter said, knowing it would be easier said than done.

The council wanted his mate pure in blood, and Becca was far from that.

He'd just have to make sure she was safe.

No matter the cost.

Chapter Six

I'm ready. I have to be."

Lily blinked at Becca's seemingly random outburst then raised a brow. Damn, Becca would have to learn to do that. She could raise both brows and look surprised, but that was about it.

"Care to elaborate on what you're ready for?" Lily asked as she placed another domino down on the table.

Becca had gone over to Lily's place under the guise of wanting to spend time with her friend, when in reality she wanted to see how a paranormal relationship would work. Okay, that wasn't quite true. She wanted to hang out with Lily anyway, but having Shade there with his black wings, tipped in blue, spread out behind him as he walked around the house helped.

Lily and Shade had been together for over a year, and already, their home looked like *theirs* rather than a mesh of a thousand-year-old angel and an OCD human-turned-brownie. Everything was in its place and at a perfect angle, but there were also antiques and other touches that must have come from Shade. In retrospect, though, those things might not have been antiques when Shade had purchased them.

It was odd and kind of exciting to hear about Shade's and Ambrose's pasts. Even Balin was much older than the girls were—just not as old as the angels. All of that made her think of Hunter and his past. She only knew the bare facts about him, his past, and his Pack.

That was something she'd have to change. Gods, she'd

been so selfish. So what if fate had decreed them perfect for each other? Did that mean she had to run away from it because it hadn't been her choice?

Hell, it *was* her choice.

Hunter was making sure of that.

"Becca? Where did you go?"

Becca shook her head to clear her thoughts at Lily's words. "Sorry. What did you say?"

Lily raised that brow again then tilted her head. "What exactly are you ready for?"

"Hunter."

A smile broke out over her friend's face before she rubbed her belly. "Yay! I'm so excited for you. I know you've been trying to hold back because you weren't sure, but I know this will work out."

Becca held her hand out at her friend's enthusiasm. "I'm not saying we're going to...mate, or whatever he calls it. I only meant that I'm going to learn about who *he* is."

Lily tilted her head, her brows bunched. "I don't understand."

"I'm saying that I've been selfish. We've spent all this time together, and all we've done is be near each other. I don't know anything about him. Not like I should."

"He's a wolf, Becca. Remember that," Shade warned as he walked into the room, his wings trailing behind him—a bad habit of his. He leaned and kissed his mate, his wife, then knelt behind her, his hand possessively on her stomach.

Gods, she hadn't realized how much she wanted that until she witnessed it firsthand.

Could she have that?

"What do you mean about Hunter being a wolf?" she finally asked.

Shade kissed Lily's temple, as if he couldn't stop himself from touching his mate. That little ball of warmth turned into jealousy, and she pushed it away.

"I know you're feeling a bit weak physically because of the

lack of a bond, but Hunter is feeling the mating urge too," Shade explained.

Becca sat up straighter. "He's in pain too."

Shade grimaced as Lily elbowed him in the stomach. "Shade, stop trying to sway her."

"I'm not, baby, but Becca needs to know the facts."

"Yes, Becca needs to know the facts," she echoed.

Gods, had she been hurting him because she needed to know more about what she wanted? Had she done exactly what she'd promised she wouldn't do?

"Hunter is a wolf," Shade continued. "He isn't like Ambrose, me, or even Balin. We might be supernaturals, but we're not human at all. We're...one with our other half."

"I don't understand."

"Hunter's wolf is part of him, but also rides him. While Balin might have the demon ride him and try to turn him, or at least that's how it was before, he was always in control. Sometimes Hunter needs to let his wolf out front and be in control. Shifters are different than other paranormals."

Becca nodded, soaking in everything she could about who Hunter or, rather, *what* Hunter was. She'd pretty much already decided to be with him, but she needed to know more.

"With that need, though, comes another side of him. He not only has to force down the bond and pull toward you with his human half, but with his wolf half as well."

"I'm hurting him?" Becca whispered. Voicing it too loudly would make it all that more real.

Shade looked pained but nodded.

Becca stood and threw her hands in the air. "Why the hell didn't he say anything?"

Shade raised a brow in similar fashion to his Lily, and Becca growled. Yes, growled. Just like the wolf-slash-man she was supposed to mate. Or, rather, wanted to mate.

"What was he supposed to say? Have sex with me and bond so we both can feel better?" Shade snorted, and Becca wanted to slap the angel who had moments ago been so nice.

Not so much now. "The unfortunate side effects on both your parts suck, I know, but really? There wasn't anything he could do. Unless you were ready for the bond, you would have just resented him the entire time. Was that really something you wanted to do?"

Becca sighed then rubbed her temples. "It's not fair. I mean, we've spent so much time together, and I know I really like him. And, yes, my body hurts, my souls hurts, and well...everything hurts to be without him because of fate and all the crap, but I wanted more time."

Lily stood up—with Shade's help—and gave her a hug. "I know, honey. I didn't know the consequences of what would happen if I slept with Shade, but you know what? I don't regret it for a minute."

"You better not, Lily."

Becca smiled as Shade growled under his breath, and Lily rubbed small circles over her baby bump.

"I'm going home to shower and pack a bag. Then I'm going to call Hunter and see if I can stay with him and his Pack. I need to know more about the wolf, not just the man."

Lily hugged her hard. "You sure you're ready for this?"

Becca let out an exasperated snort. "Really? Really. After all of this warning about hurting Hunter, you ask me if I'm ready?"

Lily kissed her cheek then tugged on the end of Becca's long red hair, making her wince at the sting. "I wouldn't be one of your best friends if I didn't make sure you weren't ready for this. You're about to give up part of your life for a man, you know, but you want to know more."

"I'm not giving up everything. Right?" Becca backed up and ran into the coffee table. She rubbed her leg, annoyed at her clumsiness. Again.

Lily gave her a small smile. "No, not everything. You're gaining so much more. Fate, though, is tricky. You're not going to be able to stay in the human realm, or at least outside the den, as much as you do now I wouldn't think. Hunter is the Beta, and

I'm pretty sure that means something more than hanging out every once in a while. You'll have to ask him. Plus, if you do mate, you're going to turn into a supernatural creature. I mean, that's the running theory anyway."

"I don't know if I'm ready to change everything like that."

"I think the lightning chose for us, dear."

Becca nodded then hugged her friend one last time. "I'm going home and showering then calling Hunter. I've made my decision, and if I keep second-guessing myself, I'm only going to hurt us more. It's not like I'm saying I'm going to actually mate with him, but I want to get closer."

Shade gave her a knowing smile then hugged her. He'd melded into their circle of friends nicely, the same as Balin and Ambrose had. Well, at least the men had made friends with most everyone. Faith would always be protective and a hard nut to crack.

Becca smiled as she drove home, thinking about the look on Faith's face when she finally found her mate. Oh, yes, that would be fun.

When she got home, she quickly packed up a bag that could last her a week then called Hunter. They might have talked every night on the phone like a couple of teenagers, but she didn't care. She loved listening to the soft growls of his voice and the deep resonating tones while he spoke. Her body would thrum for hours after speaking to him.

When she got his voicemail, she closed her eyes and let his voice wash over her. Thankfully the beep at the end was loud enough to startle her, or she would have just left a breathless moan or two on his phone.

Oh yeah, that would be a great way to start the new phase in their relationship.

"Hi, Hunter, it's Becca. I just wanted to see...uh..." Oh great, she really should have practiced this bit. "See if you minded if I went with you to the den. I want to see your place and your people, you know? I'm sorry, Hunter." She closed her eyes, willing her emotions to keep in check. "I'm sorry I've stayed away. Call me back."

She pressed *End* on her phone then stripped down to take a shower. Hopefully he'd call back soon, or she'd be stuck bouncing on her feet, all ready to leave with no place to go. Though she had a feeling Dante would be able to show her where the Pack was, she had a feeling going there unannounced with a dragon, who, for some reason, Hunter didn't care for too much, wouldn't be the best thing to do.

So instead she turned on the water as hot as it would go—which wasn't scalding or even too hot considering the age of the water heater—and left her phone on the counter in case Hunter called.

Maybe she should call again, just to hear his voice.

Okay, enough of that. Talk about becoming a stalker.

He'd call soon enough, and then the next part of her not-so-planned-out plan could work.

Becca jumped in the shower and wet down her hair, letting the water take away the aches and stresses of the day. She might have been done with school and officially a college graduate, but she still had to put in long hours at the bar to save money, though, now, after talking with Lily, she'd have to think about what she'd do.

Could she stay with Hunter half the time and stay in the human realm the other half? How did wolves make money? How did they live?

She shampooed her hair, annoyed with herself. Asking herself all those questions really didn't help matters. She needed to talk to Hunter. Even if he didn't have all the answers, at least he'd be able to help her with the easy questions.

Hunter's face was on her mind and his voice a growl that made her ache. She tried to control herself, but all she could think about was the sound of his voice and the touch of his hands and body when he'd scent-marked her.

Damn.

That had been the hottest thing ever.

She'd almost come right there, knowing he was holding

her, marking her, needing her. Her hands circled her nipples, and she imagined them being Hunter's, pinching, pulling. She gasped as she did what she wanted him to do then let her other hand fall to between her legs. Her fingers rubbed against her clit, and she moaned. Letting her one hand pinch and play with her breasts, she let her other hand spread her labia then circle her opening.

Hell, she couldn't wait to have his rough hands rasp against her skin, his forceful muscles holding her against a wall as he fucked her hard from behind.

She wasn't sweet like Lily or Nadie.

No, she wanted it rough.

She wanted Hunter.

She finger fucked herself, letting the images of Hunter wash over until her inner walls clamped around her fingers and she came. Stars burst behind her eyelids, and her legs grew heavy, weak. She leaned against the shower wall, grateful for the bath mat she'd put in the shower. Without that, she'd have fallen for sure.

The last thing she needed to explain to Hunter or the paramedics was that she'd knocked herself unconscious by fucking herself with thoughts of the man she might just have a chance with.

Oh, yes, that would go over well.

She quickly soaped herself up, being careful with the newly sensitive areas, then got out of the shower. After she dried herself off, she put on her bra and panties then her tank and an old pair of jeans. She'd get dressed up more when Hunter called, but right now, she just wanted to be comfortable.

The sound of breaking glass didn't register at first. Neither did the feel of something...off in her apartment.

Later, much too later, she turned, ignoring the hairs rising on the back of her neck, only to come face to face with a fist.

Two pairs of feet came into her line of sight and she groaned.

She hit the ground, a whimper escaping her lips, then nothing.

Becca opened her eyes but saw only darkness. She screamed, or at least tried to, but something was over her mouth. Her body shook as adrenaline surged through her, but she forced herself to calm down.

She felt the warm rush of tears spilling down her cheeks as she tried to figure out what had happened.

Two men, or at least two pairs of feet and one fist, had come into her home and taken her. She was pretty sure she had a canvas bag over her head because she could breathe, so she knew it wasn't plastic. She could feel the sharp edges of tape on her cheeks where it covered her mouth. Her hands were tied behind her back, and her legs were tied together as well.

She lay on her side, her clothes still on—thank the gods— and she knew she was in deep shit.

Hunter, Dante, Jamie, someone, please come for me.

She'd never felt so helpless in her life.

Finally the sound of footsteps reached her ears, and she stiffened. She had a feeling they weren't the steps of the cavalry, but those of the men who'd taken her.

What were they going to do to her?

"Do you know why you're here, girl?" a muffled voice asked.

She couldn't tell exactly what his voice sounded like considering she heard it through the bag and also because he must have done something to it. He almost sounded like that masked dude from *Batman*.

Didn't the man know he'd duct taped her mouth? How the hell was she supposed to answer? She didn't know why the fuck she was there.

She was glad for the tape. Knowing her, she'd say the wrong thing and end up in worse trouble.

"Her mouth is taped, you idiot," another muffled voice

spat.

Oh good, at least one kidnapper wasn't an idiot. Well, maybe.

The two men, and then a third, started yelling at each other about plans and rules, but Becca couldn't follow. Her head still ached like a bitch from the man's punch, and all she wanted to do was go home.

She had a feeling, though, that wouldn't be happening any time soon.

Oh, sweet gods, she was so not ready for this.

Why hadn't she told Hunter how she felt? For that matter, she should have thought about what she felt more. She'd been running from it because she'd been scared.

She'd always been scared.

Now she'd never have the chance to find out what Hunter looked like in his wolf form. She'd never know what she'd turn into, never find that other part of her she knew she wanted. Oh, she might be scared about the change and not want to think about it, but she wanted it.

Badly.

She'd never be able to see what Lily's baby would look like. Never hold that baby—or her own—in her arms. Never tell Dante how much he meant to her as a friend. He'd been there for her through all of her pain and her struggle to find who she was, even when she wasn't sure she'd ever get there.

She'd never be able to see Faith's reaction to finding her mate. Gods, that one hurt. Hard. She wanted to see her friend fall in love and be with the one—or two—persons who would break through her shell. In fact, Becca wouldn't be able to see any of her friends make that bond and find their inner supernatural.

She'd never see what would happen when Nadie and Dante finally found each other and figured out what the hell they were doing.

She'd never see Hunter again.

"Girl? Aren't you listening?"

Someone kicked her in the ribs, the sharp pain and crack of something snapping causing her to want to vomit.

She'd been so deep in her thoughts she hadn't been paying attention. What had she missed when she'd been acting like an idiot?

"Don't kill her yet. We need to make sure we have everything secure."

Yet?

What did they mean by yet?

"You can't be alive, girl. You shouldn't have found the Beta. Now, because he's announced his plans to mate with you, we're fucked. Can't you understand that? We can't allow this mating to take place. You have two options. We kill you now. Or you promise to stay away."

"Don't believe anything the bitch says. She's human," another voice spat.

Beta. This had to be because of Hunter. So they had plans against Hunter, and she wasn't part of them.

Well, hell.

They'd just have to get over it.

Or something.

"That bastard shouldn't have made it out of hell alive, and now look at the shit he's brought down. We'll just have to kill her. That way he'll be so despondent he'll be useless, and we can finish our plans."

Becca cried in earnest then. Gods, they couldn't kill her. They couldn't hurt Hunter. Who the hell were these people?

"We can't kill her yet. He'll know. We just have to hide her for a bit, then we can kill her."

Oh good, they'd kill her later. The sarcasm going on in her brain at the moment really wasn't helping things.

"She doesn't have to be whole to be hidden," another voice said, this one deeper, more dangerous.

They came at her as one. They kicked, punched, and clawed. She knew they were wolves and were holding their strength back from killing her, but it hurt.

She felt her skin tearing, bones breaking, bruises forming, and she couldn't fight them off.

Finally, the pain sliced through her head, and darkness came.

Well, not before she had one last thought of Hunter and how it would kill him to see this.

Then it was no more.

Chapter Seven

The fist to the face should have been the first clue something was wrong, but Hunter hadn't been thinking clearly since hearing Becca's message.

She wanted to come to the den.

She wanted to be near him and his Pack.

The joy that had spread through him at those words nearly felled him to his knees.

The fist ten minutes later almost did again.

"What the fuck?" Hunter growled at Gregory Lloyd, the council member and pain in the ass.

Lloyd struck again, but this time Hunter pulled back, catching the other man's wrist before he could contact. Lloyd snarled then tried to pull back, but Hunter tightened his grip. The other man's face blanched, the bones beneath Hunter's hand grinding.

"Why the fuck are you challenging me, Lloyd?"

The other wolf spat at him, and Hunter ducked. Now he was getting annoyed. At first, he could just call it a bad day... now? Now, he was about to kick some ass.

"I'm more dominant that you, Lloyd. You know this. We already went through this shit and did our battles over a decade ago. Why are you fighting now?"

"You don't deserve to be Beta."

Hunter blinked. The crowd he hadn't noticed gathered around them gasped. It was one thing for the council to try and get him out of his position with the initial Beta circle, but it was another to outright attack him.

"You have no say in that, Lloyd. I was nominated by *our* Alpha." He stressed the our part considering the council seemed to have a different take on what exactly it meant to be Pack. "I won the battle against your wolf. I've done all the council has required, yet you fight me on this?"

"You're nothing. You're just a lowborn wolf with a fucking human for a mate. One you haven't even shown us. What are we supposed to think? That you're actually proud of being with that bitch? No, you're shaming yourself being with her and shaming us all. The more we dilute the bloodlines, the more we dilute our power. Look around. We're nothing. We could have been so much more, but instead, we want this so-called peace?" He sneered the last word, his face red and his eyes bulging. "We have nothing. We could have been at the top of all Packs. We still *can* be."

Hunter shook his head. What the hell was the council thinking? He leaned down close to the other man's face so his voice wouldn't carry. He had a feeling that some of the stronger wolves would be able to hear, so he made it short.

"Watch your step, Lloyd. The Alpha can only handle so much disobedience then he'll have to take matters into his own hands. The council is relatively new to our culture. It can die. Just like you."

"You dare to threaten me?"

"I dare, and I'll do it one step further. You come near me, my mate, or my people, I'll gut you where you stand." Hunter had had enough of this Pack and their issues.

In his absence, most of the dominants had learned to treat submissives like shit. They were slowly starting to withdrawal completely from the human realm. Though they had Pack money and the ability to live within the den and sustain themselves for long periods of time, they still relied on the humans for most things. In fact, most wolves had human jobs and had been, before he'd been taken, completely ingrained within society.

Now they were working within the den, some never leaving excerpt in odd emergencies. Hunter was working on changing that, along with Liam and Alec, but honestly, he had no idea how to fix such a widespread issue.

Now Lloyd stood in front of him, a glare on his face, spouting shit about wanting to rule the other Packs?

How the fuck were they going to do that?

Each Pack worked on its own. There wasn't an ultimate Alpha or council. There had never been a reason to have one wolf with all that power. That much power would be too much for one man. Fuck, it was already almost too much for Josiah, hence Hunter's responsibilities.

He didn't know what Lloyd and the others had planned, but he'd have to find out soon and take care of it. He wasn't about to let anyone die or get hurt because he couldn't handle all the problems of the Pack.

This was what he wanted to bring Becca into?

She's called wanting to get to know the Pack and find out more about him—hopefully because she wanted to take one step closer to mating—but he wasn't sure he could force her into this turmoil.

Fuck.

Another fist came at his side, this time from a different person, bringing Hunter out of his thoughts. He twisted to duck the punch, but had to let go of Lloyd.

Hunter growled and let his claws break through his skin, ready to fight back.

Two of Lloyd's wolves stood by their leader's side, panting, shirtless, and looking generally fucking useless.

"I'm not going to kill you," Hunter drawled. "Not when only a beating will do." He couldn't kill them. Not outright and not right now. Technically, all Lloyd had done was try to start a battle for dominance. When the other two wolves had joined, however, it crossed the lines. Hunter could hurt them, kill them if he wanted, but as Beta, if he started killing everyone that pissed him off or wanted to try to hurt him, things would get tricky real fucking fast.

"I'm tired of having this same conversation with you," Hunter continued, keeping an eye on the growing crowd. He had a feeling that things could go badly at any moment if enough people got involved.

"Then give up and leave." Lloyd flexed his fists, looking like the strong wolf he was, but still an asshole.

Hunter snorted. "You're not very good at playing the villain, Lloyd. At least when it comes to the dialogue."

"He's just saying what we're all saying," Dorian drawled as he joined the melee.

Hunter held back his wolf, though he wanted to tear out the bastard's throat just to see if he could. Oh, yes, he could do it...and relish it.

Maybe he needed to hold back his violent tendencies for Becca.

Speaking of Becca, a spicy scent entered his nostrils then disappeared as quickly as it came. It was almost as if Becca had been standing by him...or someone who had been near her. Yet he couldn't find the scent again. Maybe he just wanted her near so much that he was imagining things.

Yes, that was a great way to prove to others he wasn't the crazy animal from hell.

"You heard what we said at last night's council meeting, yet you've done nothing to prove to us you have a mate," Dorian said. "So, tell us, where is this mystical human who has the gall to be with the big bad Beta from hell?"

Big bad Beta from Hell?

Huh, that was a new one, though he kind of liked it. Maybe he'd get it tattooed.

On Dorian's face.

"Leave my mate out of this, Dorian." The last thing he wanted to do was get Becca in the middle of anything dangerous. He'd kill for her, but he didn't want to kill in front of her. He'd already killed and shown his true side to Jamie and the others when they'd all been in hell. He could still feel the blood on his hands, the gravel and dried bones beneath his feet.

Dorian threw up his hands, his shirtless chest puffing out as he grinned like a fucking idiot. "Where is she? Is she even real? Or maybe you think you can lie to us so you don't have to mate with one of our own?"

People gasped and growled around them.

Fuck.

"I don't have to answer to you, Dorian." He bit back on the rage consuming him. He didn't want to fight. Not anymore. He'd fought all his life and would still fight to protect those he loved, but he didn't want any more blood on his hands.

"No, you have to answer to our Pack and our laws," Dorian bit out.

"My true half with be here soon."

More gasps. More growls.

"You're lying," Dorian spat, though something in the other man's voice gave Hunter pause. As if Dorian *knew* Becca wouldn't be coming to the Pack.

He shook that off and put it away for later. He couldn't completely ignore his instincts, but he'd worry about it all another time.

First he had to deal with that asshole—make that *assholes*—in front of him.

"You have to take a mate. As Beta, it's your duty to provide lineage, stability, and breeding. You've said you have a mate, yet none of us have seen this human of yours. You failed to tell Liam and Alec, your closest friends."

Hunter narrowed his eyes. He knew Liam and Alec wouldn't had said anything, yet there was no way to hide the way his friends had stiffened during the council meeting, betraying their surprise.

"You can have any of the women here. I'm sure they'd bend over for you in a minute. Just stick your dick in them and bite down to mark, and you're done."

He didn't flinch at the crudeness of Dorian's words. The women behind him though did.

"We're not here to do your bidding," one woman, a dominant wolf, shouted, and Hunter inwardly applauded.

"Yeah, he might be hot as hell, but if he has a mate? Then fuck no," another wolf put in.

The murmurs and shouts grew louder around him, and Hunter smiled. This. This was the Pack he wanted. The one that rallied together to prove they were better than the wolves Dorian and the others wanted them to be.

"Stop this, Dorian," Hunter pleaded. "You're doing no good."

Dorian grinned then turned. He pulled on a woman's arm, and she screeched. He yanked her closer to his side, and Hunter moved forward to help. Lloyd and his men moved closer, blocking his path.

Leslie, Dorian's sister—a submissive wolf—glared at her brother then gave Hunter a weak smile.

She mouthed, "I'm sorry."

Fuck. He wasn't in the mood to hear what was about to happen next.

"You won't take any of the dominant wolves? Then take Leslie. She's pureblooded and submissive. She'll do anything you want. Anything."

Dorian leered, and Hunter had to swallow down the bile rising in his throat.

"I'm not going to mate your sister, Dorian. No offense, Les."

The beautiful brown-haired wolf smiled. "None taken."

Dorian growled. "So my family isn't good enough for you?"

Leslie rolled her eyes, despite the danger she was in just being close to her brother. She had more of a backbone than most gave her credit for.

"Dorian, listen to yourself. You're reaching now. Let's stop this before it gets out of hand. I'm mating Becca, and you can't stop me."

"Really?" Dorian sneered.

The wind picked up, a slight breeze brushing Hunter's senses, and he froze.

Becca.

That spicy scent.

Tears filled Leslie's eyes. Hunter started to growl as Dorian laughed.

"What did you do? Where is she?" His voice was low, dangerous. He'd kill anyone who'd touched her.

Slowly.

"Where is who? Do you not know where your own mate is? How...unfortunate."

He glanced at Leslie's face and followed her gaze to the forest. The same area where Lloyd had a basement he used to store things for his family.

Dorian pulled on Leslie's arm, and she screamed.

"You bitch!"

"Go, Hunter!"

Hunter gave Leslie one last look and ran toward the forest, trying to pick up Becca's scent. How had Dorian gotten to her? Oh gods, what if he'd hurt her...or worse?

His wolf clawed at him then paced, growling to be let out, to be able to hunt. This time, though, it was for the man, not the wolf.

The trees passed him in a blur, her spicy scent growing stronger as he got closer to Lloyd's place. This was the man and animal he'd become.

The hunter.

He ripped the door to the underground basement off its hinges and followed Becca's scent to the lower level. Someone had cut the power, so he had only the slight light from the door he'd come through to see with. Even with his acute senses from being a wolf and the Beta, he still had to squint to see through the shadows.

"Becca?"

Damn, did his voice just crack?

He heard something move and followed the sound,

praying she was okay.

"Becca... baby, let me know where you are."

He heard a muffled moan and crept toward it. Her scent was stronger here. Finally, he saw a darker shape huddled on the floor, and he sucked in a breath.

"Oh, baby, what did they do to you?"

He crouched down beside her and slowly took off the bag over her head, holding back curses as he did it. Someone had struck her face, her sides, and who knows where else. He inhaled deeply, his body shaking as he let her scent, her fear, her relief wash over him.

He took off the tape from her mouth as carefully as he could.

"Hunter," she rasped out, the relief in her voice almost tactile.

"Oh, baby, who did this to you?" His voice was still a growl, but he tried to keep it soft.

"Hunter?" Liam and Alec stormed into the room, their wolves close to the surface. "Holy shit," Liam breathed.

"Okay, Becca, I'm going to pick you up and bring you to my home. I know this will hurt, but I need for you to be strong."

"Take me home," she whispered, her voice filled with pain.

He picked her up, wincing at her winces, and held her close to his chest. "This isn't how I wanted to show you the den."

Becca chuckled then coughed. "Don't make me laugh. It hurts."

He kissed her forehead then climbed the stairs and walked out of the basement as carefully as he could so he wouldn't jar her. He couldn't scent who had taken her. Her attackers had used perfumes and other things to mask their scents so the only one left was Becca's from when she'd been held there. He'd scented her on Dorian though, and this was Lloyd's place.

There would be justice.

There had to be.

"Watch them," Hunter ordered. Liam and Alec nodded then sank into the shadows. They'd find Leslie, protect her, and watch the others.

He made it to his home and walked to his bedroom. This hadn't been how he'd pictured bringing Becca to his home. Rage and fear warred within him, but the relief in knowing she was alive calmed his wolf.

Having her in his home in general calmed his wolf.

"What happened, Becca?"

She blinked up at him, her wide green eyes full of pain. "They took me..."

Sharp rage sliced at him, but he held back, not wanting to scare her.

"I'll kill them."

"I don't want to talk about that anymore. I'm pissed that I couldn't fight back."

Hunter frowned. "They were full-grown dominant wolves. You are human. You couldn't have fought back."

Becca scrunched her face then winced. "That doesn't make me feel any better. I don't have to make sense to be annoyed I'm not strong enough."

Hunter traced his hand along her face. His human was a bit crazy, but he liked it. "When you and I are mated, and you find your paranormal half, you'll be strong."

Worry clouded her eyes. "I called you before."

"I know, my mate."

"I wanted—"

"Let's talk about that later." He stood up and took off his shirt, watching the way her gaze followed the movement.

"What are you doing, Hunter?"

"I'm going to help you clean up, and I can't do that with my clothes on. Then I'm going to wrap that side of yours and look at your arm. I don't think it's broken actually, just bruised."

"I thought it was," she said, her eyes wide and fixed on his chest. He resisted the urge to flex. "Why are you getting naked?"

Hunter smiled. "Because I want to make sure we clean up

the dirt and grime from the basement. Plus the hot water will help your muscles relax. Don't worry, we're not going to have sex tonight."

She blinked then blushed.

She didn't have any cuts on her, so he wouldn't have to clean those. It was only the bruises, her sprained arm, and her rib that would be an issue. He left her on the bed and went to turn on the hot water. He had a large enough shower for the two of them as well as a big enough tub. He was a big guy and after fights liked to soak.

He walked back into the bedroom to find Becca lying on her side, but looking a little more relaxed.

"I'm a strong, independent woman, but right now I kind of just want you to take care of me. Okay?"

Something like pure happiness spread through him at her words. He went to her side and cupped her face. "I'll always take care of you, my Becca. That's what a mate is for. Just because you want to let me take care of you now doesn't mean you can't take care of yourself. It's about trust."

She rubbed her face on his hand, and he fell just that much more in love with her. "As long as I can take care of you too."

Images of her washing him and touching him filled his mind. "As long as you're not in danger, you're welcome to. Come on, my Becca."

He sat her up then took off her tank and bra. He couldn't help his reaction at the sight of her ample breasts and rosy nipples, but his wolf seemed to know it was the time for comfort, not need.

The bruises along her side helped tone down the edge of arousal as well.

She blushed all over, right down to those delectable nipples, but didn't say anything as he stood her up. She rested her hands on his shoulders as he took off her jeans and panties. He purposely kept his gaze from her pussy, knowing he needed to act the gentleman—even if he was a wolf.

He set her down on the bed again and stripped off his jeans. His cock was rock hard, but he ignored it. He couldn't stop his reaction to her, but he wouldn't do anything about it.

Not yet.

Hunter picked her up again and carried her to the shower. With his back to the spray, he put her down on her feet and let her lean on him.

"You're so warm," she whispered, her voice low and heavy.

"You'll be too soon."

He washed her slowly, paying careful attention to her bruises, but kept his touch easy. He didn't want to break the fragile trust she'd given him. The water trailed between her breasts, and she leaned her back against his chest. His wolf growled, content that Becca was by his side.

"Thank you for finding me. I knew you would."

"I'll always find you, Becca. I came out of hell for you."

She turned in his hold, slowly and carefully due to her ribs. "You didn't know me until after you came out of hell."

He tucked a wet strand of her fiery red hair behind her ear. "I know, but that doesn't mean I didn't come out of hell for you."

She snorted then winced. "That was the sweetest line I've ever heard."

He narrowed his eyes then leaned down to bite her lip softly. "Behave."

She gave a pointed look at his fully erect cock and raised both brows. "You first."

He pulled away, noticing the disappointment in her gaze, but forced himself to ignore it. They would have to wait to complete the bond until she felt better. Though he could tell already that whatever had made her different from normal humans—the lightning strike—was already working its magic. She was healing faster than humans, but not like a supernatural. By the morning she'd still be sore, but much better, hopefully.

Hunter turned off the water, got out of the shower, and

then gently towel-dried the both of them. "We're going to bed and can talk about everything in the morning. I have wolves I trust guarding us. You're safe here."

She nodded, her eyelids drooping. He picked her up, walked to the bedroom, and pulled back the sheets. She barely stirred when he tucked her in. He walked toward the window and looked out. Liam stood in wolf form at the edge of his property and gave a nod then went back into the shadows.

As he got into bed and pulled Becca closer, he inhaled her scent, needing it to calm down his wolf. They were safe for the moment, but that could change.

He'd find out who did this and kill them. They'd hurt what was his and deserved to pay. His Pack was dying, despite trying to grow.

He'd fix it. He'd fix it all. That's what he did.

He was the Beta.

Chapter Eight

Something warm and solid pressed against her back, and Becca never wanted to leave.

Ever.

A large callused hand spread along her belly, keeping her in place. A smile spread over her face as she rocked back, wanting to keep the dream alive. She never wanted to wake up, not when she had this heat surrounding her. The hand on her stomach slowly slid up her naked chest to cup her breast. She gasped as her nipple pebbled in his hand. Becca threw her head back, relishing in her dream lover's touch as his cock lay between her ass cheeks. If she moved slightly, he'd be able to slide right into her heat, and she'd come.

At least in her dream.

She didn't have anyone, not yet, to do this for real after all.

She moved so he could enter her, and a sharp pain rocked her chest.

Her eyes popped open, and she gasped.

Images from the day before flooded her mind, and she swallowed hard. The darkness of the basement, the sound of broken glass and deep voices all hit her system, and she bit her lip. The fear slid through her body, and then she remembered who had come for her, carrying her as though she was precious. He'd also stripped her naked and washed the night off her skin.

Hunter.

Velvet lips brushed against her neck, and she shuddered.

Okay, so it hadn't been a dream.

She could feel the heat of her skin as a blush covered her whole body.

Her whole naked body.

Pressed against Hunter's naked body.

"You've gone through the full array of emotions this morning, Becca darling," Hunter purred her in ear.

Well, maybe purred wasn't the best word for a wolf, but it was the best she could come up considering his low growl had done some very interesting things to her lady parts. She refused to come just by his voice alone. No way.

"What...what do you mean?" she asked, her voice entirely too breathy. She was already naked in bed with him. She didn't need to give him any more incentive to take her like she wanted. Yes, she knew that made no sense, but her head still hurt, and she didn't want to mate until they talked.

Damn, though, having him slide right into her dampening pussy sounded like the best possible way to wake up.

No, she would remain strong. She'd do the adult thing and talk about what exactly was happening.

Then she'd ride him like a cowgirl.

Apparently it had been too long since she'd had sex.

Way too long.

Hunter ran his lips down her neck and to her shoulder, where he bit down gently. Her body shuddered, and she arched into him. He let out a raspy chuckle then licked where he'd bitten.

"That's what I wanted from you, my mate."

"What?" Oh good, she'd been reduced to saying one word over and over.

Maybe she'd be reduced to saying yes or Hunter over and over soon.

No, down, girl.

"That sweet and spicy scent of your arousal," Hunter answered, and she blushed again. "When you woke up, or at least when you had your eyes closed, you smelled sweet enough to sink my teeth into. I wanted to bite, nibble, and lick, getting to know your taste. I wanted to lift your leg and slide into you from behind, stretching that tight pussy of yours around my cock as I rocked into you. We'd both come, and then I'd lick every inch of your skin until you were panting with need—then I'd suck your clit, your pussy, and make you come again."

Her pussy throbbed, her clit filling.

Dear. Lord.

His hand slid along her side, soothing. "Then you must have remembered where you were or how you'd come to be here because you'd stiffened, and fear seeped from your pores. I'm so sorry, Becca," he rasped out. "They shouldn't have come after you because of who I am. I'd say that I'd let you walk away from all of this, but I'd be lying."

He pulled her underneath him so his forearms were on either side of her head, his long hair brushing her face as he hovered over her. He'd made sure that their bodies didn't touch though, as if he knew that as soon as that happened, there'd be no going back.

"I'm not letting you go, Becca. We might be in the early stages of mating, but I refuse to let you go. Not until you know who I am. Not until I know who you are. I don't want to let you go."

She gulped. "Even if I begged for you to let me go?"

Pain flashed across his face before he schooled his features. "If you desired to go...I'd follow your wishes because I cannot bear to hurt you, but I'd do all in my power to convince you to stay."

She reached up and cupped his face, the bristles on his cheeks rubbing along her palm. "I don't want to go."

A shudder racked his body, and he turned to kiss her palm.

"We need to talk first."

He nodded then leaned to kiss her lips softly. Before she could savor the velvet of his lips, he pulled back. "I want you to heal first as well, my Becca."

His words brought back her pain, but not as much as she'd thought she'd have. "Why aren't I hurting more?"

Hunter brushed a lock of hair behind her ear then moved off of her, leaving her feeling oddly bereft at the loss. "I think it's because you're healing faster than a normal human," he answered as he strode naked to his dresser, where he pulled out a pair of jeans.

She couldn't keep her gaze off his fully erect cock—oh Lord—or his ass.

He looked edible.

Absolutely fucking edible.

And hers if she wanted.

Oh how she wanted. That wasn't the issue, not anymore. She wanted him, but she wanted to make sure they talked first. She didn't just want to jump into bed with him—more than she already had—without knowing what he was thinking.

His words pulled her away from his now covered cock and to his face. She sat up, wincing slightly, pulling the sheet up to cover her breasts. "I'm not human?"

She looked down at the fading bruises on her arms and gasped. She didn't look like anything but herself, but she was definitely not healing like a human. "What does this mean?"

Hunter ran a hand through his hair then shrugged, the muscles in his arms and chest moving in such a way that had Becca closing her legs.

Damn, the man was hot.

He gave her a knowing smile, and she rolled her eyes. The dude had to know he was hot. "I think you're healing faster because whatever happened to you in that bar the night the storm changed you. Yes, it takes completing the mating bond with your true half for that part of your DNA to become prominent so you can actually change, but things might be different now."

"Then why didn't Lily and Jamie heal quickly when they were attacked? Why didn't I heal when the djinn attacked us?"

Hunter growled at the reminder of her being skewered to

a wall, and she didn't blame him. It wasn't something she liked to remember either. "Those weren't superficial things. I think that given enough time, the cuts and scrapes would have healed on their own. You don't have any broken bones, and I think your rib is only bruised, not broken. The others, though, they had life-threatening injuries. As did you that night."

She nodded, trying to absorb the information. So much had changed that night. They still didn't know *why* they'd been chosen. Nor did they know if they'd all change into something once they found their mates, though it seemed likely. They also didn't know if they'd be long-lived or, now, heal. It was all up in the air, but they were learning more every day.

"Plus, Becca, you all react to your true halves differently. It would make sense that you'd all have different changes as well. It could be due to the fact you all might be separate paranormals, or it could be that you're all just different people in general."

She blew the hair from her face. "I just hate not knowing."

He walked toward her and sat at the edge of the bed then tucked that piece of hair behind her ear again. "I know. I hate not knowing too. We'll take it one step at a time, okay?"

She nodded, knowing they didn't have another choice.

"Wait. I need to call my friends to let them know I'm okay."

Hunter nodded. "I've already had Liam and Alec, my friends, call Dante." He growled the dragon's name, and Becca barely resisted the urge to roll her eyes. It wasn't as if Hunter had anything to be jealous about, but she'd let him have that growly voice since it was hot as hell.

"So they know I'm safe?"

"Yes, they wanted to come here and get you out considering who'd taken you in the first place, but Dante persuaded them to let you stay here." His eyes glowed, and she blinked. That was new.

"Why are your eyes glowing, and why did Dante tell them

to let me stay?"

Hunter pulled out a pair of sweats and a shirt from his dresser and placed them on the bed. "I don't have anything else for you to wear right now. I'm sorry. These will have to do."

"That's fine, now answer my questions." She got dressed under the covers, and Hunter smirked. He might have already seen—and touched—the goods, but she needed to retain her modesty every once in a while.

"Dante told them to let you stay because, if you were to leave right now, my wolf would go crazy. I need you here, Becca. I can protect you better if you're by my side. Plus, I just want to be with you."

Her heart melted at that thought, and she wanted to wrap her arms around him. She held back.

Barely.

"My eyes glow when I'm angry or feel another heightened emotion like arousal. So when I'm coming, my wolf will rise to the surface, and my eyes will glow. When I'm talking about the soon-to-be-dead men who took you, I get fucking pissed, and I can't control my wolf as well, hence the glow."

She let the coming part slide since she wanted to talk about other important things first, and if she talked about sex, she wasn't sure if she could stop herself from rubbing all over him like a cat in heat.

Again with the cat references, she needed to think of better dog—or wolf—ones.

"You can't kill people if you don't know who did it."

"I know who did it," Hunter said, the certainty in his voice like a solid presence.

"You do? For sure?" That sickly sense of fear wrapped around her spine, and she hated herself for it. Though she'd felt something like it before, it had been for her friends, not her. She didn't like feeling weak. She *wasn't* weak. She didn't want to have to wait and have the handsome hero sweep her up in his arms and save her.

That had been what happened though.

She'd been weak because she'd been human.

That would change soon though.

She wouldn't be weak anymore.

She *couldn't* be weak anymore.

"I know who took you, though, right now, we can't prove it. They covered their scents, and though Leslie, the sister of one of the captors, would defend us, I don't want to risk her safety."

Something like jealousy swept through her, and she hated herself for it.

Hunter raised a brow. "I think of Leslie like a sister. Her brother, Dorian, is a sadistic bastard, and I don't want her to be punished for speaking out."

Becca nodded, relived and a little ashamed for even thinking that Hunter would want another, and even though he was old enough to have a past, it didn't make it any better for her.

Great, now she was a jealous girlfriend.

Or mate.

Whatever.

"Liam and Alec are working on finding evidence so we can retaliate. Because I'm the beta, I can't take on the council members without proof. If I were to do so, it would be detrimental to the Pack right now."

Becca shook her head, confused.

"Okay, you need to explain all of that. The only thing I know about how wolves work comes from TV and romance novels."

Hunter quirked a smile, though she could still see the stress lines in the corners of his eyes. "Get out of bed while I make us something for breakfast. We can talk while we eat."

Becca looked down at the baggy shirt and sweats. Yeah, she really wasn't oozing sex appeal at the moment, and she really had to use the restroom. Plus, there was the whole morning-breath issue.

"Uh, do you have a spare toothbrush?" He'd already kissed her that morning, and with his heightened senses, she was a little surprised he hadn't passed out already.

Hunter smiled full-out, his white teeth stark against his honey-dipped skin.

Oh, he was pretty.

"No, Liam and Alec are bringing things from your apartment a bit later though. You can use my toothbrush. It's not like we haven't been kissing."

"That's kind of gross. Wait, they're going to my place? Without me there? I don't want them touching my underwear."

Hunter growled. "They won't be touching your underwear. Faith is meeting them there to pack your belongings. I wasn't sure you'd approve of two men you didn't know in your place, plus I don't want them touching anything of yours they don't have to. If any man is going to touch your underwear, it's going to be me."

Becca relaxed at the thought of Faith being there; at least her friend would make sure she got everything she needed. She held back a laugh at the thought of tough-as-nails Faith with anyone though. "Uh, do the guys know Faith's...uh, personality?"

Hunter grinned. "Since Liam and Alec are my best friends, yes, I warned them. And, no, Faith isn't coming here. I don't want to introduce her, or anyone else, to the Pack when we're still in flux. I want to make sure you're safe first. Why is sharing a toothbrush with me gross?"

Becca rolled her eyes. "Never mind. I'll meet you in the kitchen."

She scurried off to the bathroom and closed the door behind her. When she looked at her reflection in the mirror, she couldn't hold back the groan.

Sexy, she was not.

Her red curls stood on end—that damned lock that Hunter kept playing with in her face again. The bruises from her attack were fading at least, but since she'd gone to bed with wet hair, she looked like a zombie freak.

Okay, maybe that wasn't the best description, but it was

the closest.

The dark circles under her eyes and paleness of her skin had more to do with the weakness from not mating with Hunter than her ordeal, she thought, but they didn't really make her look her best.

Not that she was vain or anything, but at least not looking like crap would have been nice.

She quickly took care of the necessities, brushed her teeth with this toothbrush anyway, and tried to manage her curls. Hopefully Liam and Alec—whom she'd only met vaguely—would be back with her things soon.

Though she'd have preferred to wear her own things, she kind of liked wearing Hunter's clothes. It made things that much more...intimate. Plus, she had a feeling he liked having his scent all over her. At least that's what she thought considering how he'd reacted with Jason and the whole scent-marking thing.

She walked through Hunter's place, taking in the warm tones and lived-in feeling of his home. It wasn't a bachelor pad, but a place where she could tell Hunter felt comfortable. Plus, there was room to grow a family.

She froze.

Okay, she needed to backtrack that thought a bit.

Becca followed the scent of bacon into the kitchen and about passed out. Hunter stood in front of the stove cooking bacon and eggs, naked but for a pair of well-worn jeans that made his ass look like heaven.

"Aren't you afraid of the splatter on your chest?" she blurted out then closed her eyes.

She'd have wished for a hole to open up and swallow her, but since Jamie had already been to hell, she didn't want to risk the whole fire and brimstone thing.

Hunter turned his head, a grin on his face. "It'll only burn a little while."

She rolled her eyes. "So manly of you."

"I try. As for the grease, I move away before it burns me. Fast reflexes and all."

"Huh, I never thought of that. Good to know. Oh, and that smells heavenly."

He reached out for her, and she moved into his arms without another thought. She fit perfectly against his side—something she'd known already, but loved to think about anyway. He gave a kiss to the top of her head, and she sighed.

She was a goner.

"Breakfast is almost ready. You want to get the milk or juice out of the fridge?"

She squeezed him then pulled away, knowing the act of domesticity was a little too perfect, but she liked it. "What are you in the mood for?"

He raised a brow at her words, and she blushed. "Not *that*. You know what I mean. Juice or milk?"

"Milk works for me. I have the coffee going too."

"I love coffee. I'm an addict." She got the milk out for the both of them to go with their coffee since she figured she needed the calcium to heal. Or she could just be making up things as she went along, but she'd go with it.

"Good to know," Hunter said as he plated their meals, and then he walked to the table. Her gaze followed the way the long lines of his body moved, and she had to tear her eyes away.

Answers first.

Sex later.

Maybe.

They ate in silence for a minute or two. Hunter looked like the wolf he was—ravenous—while Becca herself just about died of bliss as she bit into a slice of bacon.

Yes, she was a bacon addict, but she didn't care.

"You want me to tell you about the Packs now?" Hunter asked before taking a drink of his milk. Becca watched the way his throat worked as he swallowed, and she almost fanned herself.

She needed to get a grip on her lust.

Fast.

"Please, and not just because I'm here now. I had wanted

to know before. I mean, when we were going on those dates, I saw a glimpse of the man, but I want to know the wolf too."

Hunter smiled, and she held off swooning.

"Each Pack has an Alpha and a Beta. The Alpha, Josiah, leads the Pack but isn't as vocal as the Beta. Josiah has to deal with the other Packs more than I do. He also holds the Pack together because of his strength. The Beta, me, deals with the day-to-day things in the Pack. It's my job to make sure the members of the Pack are treating each other with respect and according to hierarchy and to make sure there isn't an internal resistance."

Becca nodded, absorbing everything he said.

"There's also the council." His voice dropped to a low growl at that, and she instinctively reached out to hold his hand. He squeezed back then continued. "The council is made up of the five leading families of the Pack. Not all Packs have councils. Our council's job is supposed to ensure the Pack's safety and adherence to the rules that govern us all. However, that isn't happening. Liam and Alec are council members and are the only things holding back the council from utter ruin. The other three, Dorian, Gregory, and Alistair, want to take over the Pack. They want to make the Pack a democracy or at least change out the Alpha. Wolves don't work like that, and it's hurting our Pack because of it."

Becca nodded, tightening her grip on Hunter's hand. "Those three are the three you think took me, right?"

Hunter nodded, a low growl coming from this throat. "Yes. They'll pay. For that and more."

"More?"

"Liam, Alec, and I think they are the ones who sent me to hell."

Becca gasped. "You think the wolves betrayed you? I hadn't thought about why you were there in the first place." She lowered her gaze. Why hadn't she thought that someone had sent him there?

"I wasn't there of my own accord. I woke up there one

morning, as if someone had come into my room and taken me away. I don't remember it all. As the Beta of the Pack, I should have been stronger than that, but I don't know what happened."

Becca stood up and wrapped her arms around him, needing to comfort when she didn't know how.

He pulled her onto his lap, inhaling her scent. She could feel the rapid pace of his heartbeat against her side, and she cuddled harder.

"When I was gone, my younger brother, Samuel, took over my job. They killed him because I wasn't here."

Becca swallowed hard, tears threatening to form. "I'm so, so sorry, Hunter."

She kissed him softly, putting all the emotion, care, and what could be love, in the kiss. He held her close, kissing her back with utter care, and it almost broke her.

"I'll find a way to prove all of this. I'm sorry for bringing you into a war you weren't ready for."

"Hunter, I wasn't ready for anything, but I know I can handle it if you're by my side."

He kissed her again, and that heat from low in her belly rose again, consuming her.

Hunter growled softly. "You should get off my lap if you don't want to finish this, my Becca."

She looked into those yellow eyes of his and licked her lips. "I know that I can't go back to who I was. I don't know what I'll be or *who* I'll be when things change, but I'm ready to be by your side if it happens."

Hunter growled softly. "There's something you need to know. As Beta, I'm required to take a mate. I don't want you to think I'm taking you because the council tells me I have to. I want you, Becca."

It might have been the pull of the bond that hadn't yet formed, or it might have been just fate itself, but she didn't care. She wanted this man, this wolf.

"You're mine, Hunter."

He grinned a feral smile then pulled her closer. "As you're

mine."

Chapter Nine

The taste of Becca on Hunter's tongue was pure bliss. She sat on his lap, his cock pressed against her ass, and he wanted to keep her flavor forever. She wiggled in his hold, and he groaned, his cock aching at the contact.

He pulled back, breathless. "If you keep wiggling like that, I'm going to come, and it'll ruin my reputation."

She raised both brows—he loved that she couldn't raise one a time, though she tried. "You have a reputation? Should I ask?"

He bit her lip, hard, then soothed the sting with his tongue. The little gasp from both actions went straight to his dick. He held back a groan and adjusted himself. "No one matters except you."

"Good answer, boyo."

He grinned then moved her so she straddled him, his cock directly against her heat, only his jeans and the sweats she wore between them. She threw her head back and sighed at the contact. Since she'd left her throat so vulnerable, he couldn't resist leaning forward and licking down her neck, biting down softly at the juncture.

A shiver went through her body, and he growled. "I'll mark you here a bit later when I'm balls deep in that pussy of yours, your inner walls clamping around me as you milk my cock. Then we'll be mated in truth, our bond cemented."

She lowered her head, her gaze glassy already. "That should sound odd, but damn, I want you to bite me."

"My pleasure."

He wrapped her hair around his fist and pulled. She let out a little gasp that again went straight to his cock then rocked against him. He pulled her head to the side and sucked on her neck, needing her taste forever on his tongue. He could feel her scorching heat through his jeans and knew she was ready to come as soon as he touched her, but he didn't want her to go just then. No, he wanted to tease.

Hunter stood with her still in his arms, his hands on her ass, and she gasped. "Where are you taking me?"

"You'll see," he growled.

He sat her on the edge of the table and pulled her shirt up over her head. She barely had any time to react before his mouth was on her nipple, sucking the tight bud between his teeth.

"Jesus, Hunter. You don't pull any punches, do you?" Her breath quickened as she spoke, and he could scent her arousal.

Oh yes, his little mate wanted this. Badly.

He slid her nipple out of his mouth then kissed between her breasts. "I never pull punches. It's who I am, my Becca. I'm a wolf. I fight, fuck, and do everything balls out."

She gasped at his words, pushing her chest up ever so slightly that he just *had* to lick and suck on her other nipple. Come on, it was *right* there. She tasted of berries, sweet, delicious berries. He'd never thought nipples or any person could taste so sweet, but hell, this was manna.

He felt her fingers tangle through his hair, pressing him closer to her breasts, and he smiled. She wiggled against him so he pulled back, needing to see the desire in her eyes.

He wasn't disappointed.

Dark pools of heat and lust filled her pupils, letting only a small rim of green remain. He couldn't wait to make her lose it all. She would fall to her knees, and shake with release.

He quickly divested her of the sweats she wore, loving that she raised her bottom for him as if she couldn't wait any more.

Neither could he.

Then he knelt between her legs and spread her knees apart.

"Hunter..."

"Shh, Becca, let me."

He saw her nod from of the corner of his eye, but didn't let his gaze leave her pussy—so wet, so pink, so...his.

He just had to take a taste.

He licked around the edges of her pussy, letting his tongue dart into her heat then back out again so he'd tease and tempt. He let his hands slide up her thighs then put one hand on her hip to keep her steady and let the other slide to her pussy. He pressed his thumb on the hood of her clit then rubbed hard circles around it, not touching it directly. She moaned and tried to push closer, but his other hand kept her still.

"Hunter, please, it's too much."

"Not yet, Becca," he groaned, sucking and licking her pussy. Fuck, her juices tasted even sweeter than her nipples— like honeyed syrup, perfect for his tongue.

He flicked her clit once, loving the way her ass shot off the table, then pressed her hip down again before rubbing harder around her clit. He repeated this process over and over, keeping his mouth on her pussy, and finally, she came hard against his face.

She screamed his name, her inner walls clamping around his tongue, and he continued to lick, needing her to be on edge again before he did anything else. She squirmed, and he lapped up all her juices, not wanting to miss a drop.

He finally kissed the inside of both thighs then stood on shaky legs. His cock strained his zipper, and he had a feeling if he didn't take them off he'd have permanent teeth marks on his dick.

"Dear. Lord."

Hunter chuckled at her breathless words then scooped her up and took her to the bedroom. She lazily wrapped her arms around his neck and rested her head on his shoulder. He fell just a little bit more in love with her easy trust, and his wolf prowled below the surface needing to mark and mate.

He set her on the edge of the bed then stripped out of his jeans. His cock bobbed against his belly, and he smiled at Becca's wide-eyed reaction.

"Is that all mine?" She smiled but didn't move her gaze from his dick.

Hunter threw his head back and laughed then walked toward her and cupped her face, forcing her gaze to his.

"All yours. Everything I have is yours, baby."

She grinned then leaned forward, licking the head of his cock.

A jolt of lust zipped down his spine, and he groaned. "Holy fuck, okay, don't do that. If you touch me, I won't last much longer, and I need to mark you. Now."

Her mouth quirked in a smile, and she leaned back on her forearms, her breasts bouncing a bit as she did so.

"You're no fun."

Hunter narrowed his eyes and let out a soft growl. "I'll show you fun, Becca mine."

Carefully, in case she still was sore, he quickly sat on the edge of the bed and moved her to his lap so she faced him. Her knees were on either side of his thighs, her pussy sliding against his cock. He'd been through torture before, but this sweet, exquisite version had to be his favorite.

She placed her hands on his shoulders, her gaze never leaving his.

"Are you ready for this?" he asked. Even though it might kill him to stop, he would. This wasn't going to be a normal coupling. No condoms between them and birth control wouldn't work on their first mating, not when more was at play than just simple biology. If fate wanted a baby to come from their bond, then it would.

Soon he'd sink in teeth into her shoulder, and they'd bond fully, becoming mates for life, not something that could be changed or taken lightly. He wanted this more than anything, more than he'd thought. The council might want him to find a mate, but he'd wait longer to form the bond if that was what Becca wanted.

This coupling would also show Becca her new paranormal side, something scary as hell to a human, he would think.

Everything would be different.

He didn't care.

He wanted her, and he hoped to the gods she wanted this, wanted him.

Becca moved her hands up his shoulders to frame his face. "I want this. I want a future. Let me love you, Hunter."

He sucked in a breath at her words then gripped her hips to raise her into position. With their gazes locked, he slowly slid her down. She gasped, her eyes widening, her breath coming in pants at the intrusion. His breathing matched hers as her silky heat surrounded his cock in beautiful agony.

Finally she sat on his thighs, skin to skin, his cock fully in her pussy. He let her sit there for a moment while they both adjusted to the feeling. He had to concentrate hard not to come right there.

"Ride me, Becca."

She blinked then slowly smiled. "I figured you'd be the guy who wanted control."

He growled softly and nipped her lip. When her pussy tightened around his dick, he sucked in a breath. His little mate liked to be bitten.

Good to know.

"I love control. I'll have all of it. Right now, though, I want to watch you ride me. I want to watch your breasts bounce as you move. I want you to come around my cock, your juices sliding around us, slippery and wet. Then, only then, will I take back control and fuck you hard and long before mating you."

"Yes," she whispered.

He grinned then sucked in a breath as she moved. She rolled her hips then slid up and down his length. Hunter ran his hand up her side then cupped her breast, even as she moved, needing to touch her. She rode him hard, and he concentrated on her breasts and her pleasure so he wouldn't come. As a wolf, he could go more than once in a bout of sex, but he wanted to come for the first time as he marked her.

Call him sentimental.

Becca closed her eyes as she rode him, and he slid his hand down her belly to stroke her clit. With just that one movement she was off again, coming hard around his cock.

He gritted his teeth so he wouldn't come in her tight pussy. Her body shook, her head thrown back, and fuck, she was the most beautiful thing he'd ever seen. While she was still riding her high, he pulled out then set her on her knees on the bed. She was still falling to the bed as he pumped into her from behind.

"Holy shit," she breathed.

He smiled then gripped her hips, pistoning into her. She leaned forward and gripped the bed sheets, and his gaze followed the long line of her back. Sweat broke out over each of them, but still, he fucked her hard.

No, not fucked, this was something more. He already felt the connection brewing, already felt the heat that was something more than just a chemical reaction.

This...this was everything.

He pumped into her, and she moved her ass back, as if needing more of him. Tingles started at the base of his spine, and his balls tightened. He knew he didn't have much time until he came.

He leaned forward so his chest lay against her back. She turned her head, and he captured her lips in a scorching kiss.

"Mine," he growled.

"Yours," she whispered, her gaze glassy.

He pumped into her one more time, hard, then bit into her shoulder. She cried out in bliss, and he came.

He jetted into her pussy, his cock throbbing, and he felt the mating bond snap into place. It wasn't a bond that gave them the other person's innermost thoughts and feelings, but rather a solid connection to another being.

Hunter slid his teeth out of her shoulder then licked the wound. She'd already started healing at his touch, but the mark would be there forever. He moved to lay on his side, his cock still deep within her, and pulled Becca close to his chest.

"Becca?"

"I'm here," she mumbled, her voice heavy, soothing.

"Are you okay?" He knew he'd been rough, but hell, he hoped he hadn't hurt her.

"I'm...perfect," she whispered, and he could sense the smile in her voice.

He smiled back, content for the first time in forever, and kissed her mating mark.

She gasped at the sensation, and he licked the mark again.

"Stop doing that. I can't come again."

He chuckled but moved his lips back, not wanting to overwhelm her more than he already had.

He pulled out of her and almost had her turned to face him when she froze, her spine stiffening.

"Becca?"

He quickly leaned over her as her body started to shake, her eyes rolling back in her head.

"Becca!"

She seized beneath him, and her body started to glow with golden hue that quickly changed to a green hue and back again. He pulled her close so she wouldn't hurt herself.

Fuck.

Ambrose and Balin had mentioned that the change would happen right after she made love with her true half, but he hadn't expected it to be this dramatic...this painful for her. What had he done? He hadn't wanted to hurt her, and now look at what was happening.

After what seemed like an eternity, she stopped seizing, and the golden and green glow faded. He pushed her hair back from her face and looked over her body for any signs of injury or what she had turned into, but he couldn't tell anything.

He took a deep breath, and her spicy scent mingled with something new filled his nostrils. He frowned then leaned to take another breath.

Leprechaun.

His mate was a leprechaun.

He smiled at the thought.

Well, that was new.

Becca fluttered her eyelashes then stared at him. "What happened?"

Hunter kissed her softly, needing to reassure himself that she was okay.

"We bonded, and you changed, sweetie."

She swallowed hard then looked down at herself, well, what parts she could see as he was still currently leaning over her.

"What am I? I don't see anything different."

Hunter smiled then sat between her legs so he could pull her onto his lap. She leaned into his hold, and he gripped her tighter. "You're a leprechaun."

Becca pulled back and blinked. "You mean the little dude on the cereal box who has a pot of gold, likes rainbows, and is lucky?"

Hunter snorted. "No, not like that, the same way I'm not some angsty teen or some weird half man-half wolf movie reject."

Becca laughed, and some of the tension eased from her— precisely what he'd wanted.

"So what does this mean? Why aren't I different? I feel kind of like I've been gypped or something. Lily and Jamie have awesome new looks, and I'm still me."

His grip tightened, and he kissed her hard. "You're still you, and I like the way you are. Leprechauns, like all paranormals, are different. You'll glow gold when you have heightened emotions, so we'll have to control that. You'll also have a little bit of magic, I think. We'll have to ask around about that. Oh, and you'll be able to teleport."

He grinned as her eyes widened at that last remark.

"Really? Hell yeah. The other girls can't do that last part."

"See? You'll like it." Though he'd kind of wished she'd end up as a shifter of sort, this new development was nice. He'd be able to help her through every step as she learned who and what she was. As her mate, he'd be by her side and be her protector.

His wolf paced inside him, eager to protect, but happy at her safety nonetheless.

When Becca learned control, she'd be able to protect herself better as well. She'd not only be able to teleport away from danger, but also use her strength to fight back. The other wolves wouldn't be able to harm her when he couldn't be by her side.

He calmed at that last bit.

Yes, this was for the best.

"What about my luck though?" she asked. "I mean, I trip over everything in my path and run into walls and doors more often than not. How the hell am I supposed to be this lucky gold thing?"

Hunter snorted. "Baby, I think you're just a klutz. I don't think being a leprechaun will have any impact on that."

Becca narrowed her eyes then leaned forward to bite his lip. He stiffened, aware that she'd behaved as his mate, playful and territorial.

His wolf howled, and he almost joined in.

Oh yes, he was going to like being mated.

Hunter framed her face and brought her lips to his. Gods, he'd wanted this woman, and now she was his. His wolf loved her already. She might have been weaker than him, but her spirit was strong. The man though... did he love her? Hunter knew he wanted her, admired her, respected her, and liked her. It was a given, though. Right?

He had a feeling he was well on his way to being fully in love with her.

This was his mate, his future, his life.

He'd do everything and anything to protect her.

Even fight the Pack he'd fought so hard to come back to.

Chapter Ten

If one more person bumped into him and Becca again, Hunter might have to growl at his Pack mates.

Again.

Walking around the den should have literally been a walk in the park.

Not so much.

"Why are they all still staring at me?" Becca asked as she leaned into his side.

Hunter narrowed his eyes at some of the wolves who couldn't keep the fascination of the Beta's new mate off their faces. It had been a little over a month since they'd bonded, and the Pack hadn't yet gotten used to her daily presence.

The two of them had fallen into a routine of sorts within the Pack. In other words, they spent most of their time in bed, on the couch, in the shower, or on the table letting the mating urge ride them. They also got to know each other a bit more, though he knew Becca had more to tell him about her past.

That would come though.

They hadn't left the den, even though he'd wanted to make sure she knew she had a choice. She'd insisted on staying there to get to know how his world worked. She wanted to immerse herself with the wolves and learn all she could. Then later, she promised, they'd go back to the human world where he could learn about *her* life. Dante had already promised that he'd take care of her job and home, so that hadn't been an issue. Though her friends missed her, he knew they'd welcome her back as soon as she was ready.

Big changes like a new mating, new species, and being kidnapped required time to adjust, and he had a feeling she wasn't ready to face her friends with all of it until she was settled. His job was to make sure she felt safe while she focused, and so far, it was working.

Soon though, they'd go to the human realm, and he'd have to be the one who got stares and odd looks.

He'd be ready as long as Becca was by his side.

Becca had also made friends with Liam, Alec, and, not surprisingly, Leslie. He'd had a feeling Leslie would be part of their lives, even if it was in a little sister role. Leslie might have been a couple decades older than Becca, but Becca had taken to the elder sister part seamlessly. Dorian, though, had been an issue. Not a big one considering the three council members were keeping things quiet recently, but an issue nonetheless. The wolf didn't like sharing his sister and, frankly, was treading on thin ice.

Liam, Alec, and Hunter hadn't been able to prove the council members had anything to do with Becca's kidnapping. All they'd collected was a mix of tainted scents and the fact that they'd been in Lloyd's basement. However, since Lloyd had technically abandoned the shelter years ago, according to him, *anyone* could have broken in and used it to frame him.

Hunter couldn't deliver justice if he had no proof. The Pack wouldn't stand for it, not when they were already in turmoil and unsettled.

"Hunter?"

Becca's voice brought him out of his thoughts, and he leaned to kiss her temple. She moved into his side and shuddered.

"They're staring because they're jealous that I have you and they do not."

Becca snorted then rolled her eyes. "Sure, honey, and after that I'll go have tea with the Easter bunny." She paused. "Wait, are there bunny shifters?"

The person passing them gave her a look as if Becca were crazed but laughed with Hunter anyway.

"No, no prey shifters. Only predators." Well, as far as he knew. There *could* have been more out there considering most paranormals were very secretive about who they were and what they could do, but Hunter didn't think that was the case here.

"Come on, you know it would have been cute to see little tiny bunnies with pointy teeth."

Hunter rolled his eyes. "You've been watching far too many movies that provide you with unrealistic expectations. Plus, if there *were* bunny shifters, I'd have found them. After all, bunnies taste amazing."

Becca froze then hit him hard on the arm. Others looked at her as though she was crazy for hitting the Beta, but they'd get over it. She was his mate, so she could do anything she wanted to him, as long as he got to sleep by her side at night.

"That is *so* not funny, Hunter Brooks. I can't believe you'd eat Thumper."

"I ate Bambi and his mother too," he deadpanned.

Becca stuck her finger in her mouth and pretended to gag. "Thank the gods I didn't turn into a shifter." She winced and looked around her. "I'm just saying I couldn't stomach it. Sorry, I love you guys."

Most of the wolves around her just laughed, knowing what she meant. A few others though, the wolves on Dorian's side, glared. However, they always glared, so this wasn't new.

"You'd get used to hunting if you were a wolf," Liam drawled as he came to their side, Alec right behind him.

Becca stuck out her tongue then held open her arms. Liam stepped right into them and gave her a hard hug. Alec's hug was a bit softer, but just as brotherly. Hunter didn't have a problem with either of his friends hugging or touching her, as long as they kept it platonic. They were Pack, and the closest of his friends, so it only made sense that they would want to bring Becca into their folds. Becca seemed to love it, and he could tell from her scent it was just like she was hugging Dante or Shade or the triad—she just liked having friends.

It occurred to Hunter he might have to apologize to the dragon for his attitude, but he knew it wouldn't happen. Hunter was just a little too dominant to deal with bowing down to a dragon.

Even one who happened to be best friends with his mate.

"I still don't know how to use magic or teleport," Becca said. "Let me deal with that first, then maybe I'll get used to you guys eating baby bunnies."

Liam placed his hand over his chest and feigned shock. "We never said *babies*."

Hunter pulled Becca into his arms and kissed the top of her head. "We don't eat babies, you dork."

She tilted her head so she could smile at him, and he laughed. "Oh, I know. I just like seeing Liam overreact."

Alec rolled his eyes. "He does that often."

"I do not," Liam grumbled, folding his arms over his chest.

Hunter just shook his head and hugged Becca tighter. He knew they should move to the side and get out of the way, considering standing around in the middle seemed a bit odd, but he didn't feel like moving. They might have been in the center of the den with people walking around them, but he didn't care if he was displaying more affection than normal. He had his mate in his arms and his best friends by his side.

What more could he want?

"There's that delectable mate of yours," a voice said from behind them.

Hunter growled, turning toward Dorian and pulling Becca behind him. Physically, she might have been stronger than she had been as a human, but she still couldn't control all her new strengths and powers yet. Nor did she even know what they all were. So far all she could do was open a jar of garlic with more ease and pick up pieces of furniture with relative ease. Those powers, however, fluctuated in strength as she was learning how to use them.

It had been an experience.

They were planning on meeting with her new people and council soon so she could learn. That, however, wouldn't do them any good at the moment.

"What do you want, Dorian?" he asked, his voice as calm as he could make it.

Dorian smirked like the bastard he was then raised a brow. "All I'm doing is complimenting that mate of yours. After all, we, the council, *were* the ones who told you to mate with her in the first place."

Becca's grip tightened on his hand, and he had to hold himself back from killing Dorian right then and there. Thankfully Hunter had explained to Becca beforehand what exactly Dorian meant by that, but it still didn't help matters. He knew Becca had issues with dealing with fate's hand in their mating, let alone a council of overbearing wolves who had an ulterior motive—Liam and Alec excluded, of course.

Becca leaned around him, causing his wolf to rise to the surface, angry she'd put herself in any form of danger. "Thanks for the compliment, I guess. However, I know you had nothing to do with our mating other than trying to get in the way of it. So...thanks. Are we done?"

Hunter smiled and squeezed his mate's hand as he pushed her behind him. He liked this feisty side of her. She might not be a wolf and have the ability to play the dominance game, but she wasn't a pushover by any stretch of the word.

Gods, he loved her.

He'd tell her that...eventually.

Dorian's smirk lost some of its edge, and fury filled his gaze. Alec and Liam stood on either side of Hunter, still protecting Becca, but their Beta as well. Hunter didn't want this to come down to a fight, but he might not have another choice, not when Dorian was as volatile as he was.

"Your little leprechaun won't be able to hide behind your skirts for long," Dorian spat. "Remember, she'll have be strong to act like the Beta's mate. If not..." The other wolf shrugged.

Hunter's muscles bunched, ready to attack the bastard. "If not, well, I guess fate will have to provide another mate for you. After all, what use is a dead mate?"

Hunter sprang, his claws digging into Dorian's shoulder before the other wolf could blink. Hunter had his other hand wrapped around the bastard's throat, careful not to cut him and cause the man to bleed out too quickly.

Dorian swallowed hard, that bit of fear not easily hidden until he blinked, fury replacing it. "Temper, temper," Dorian choked out.

"Come near her again and I'll gut you where you stand. You're only living now because you're council." Even that wasn't holding Hunter back too much anymore. The idea that the council thought they could attack his mate and hold her captive made his skin crawl. The council had too much power, and Hunter couldn't take it anymore.

He might tear down the fabric of their Pack by defeating the council, but it was in their best interest.

He just hoped the Pack saw it that way.

He released Dorian, letting the other wolf fall to his knees then rise up. "Go home, Dorian."

Dorian snorted then walked away, his buddies trailing after him like lost puppies.

Small arms wrapped around his waist, and he let Becca's scent wash over him. She calmed his wolf even through the darkest haze.

"Let's go home," she whispered. "I'd rather just be in your arms than out right now."

He turned and lifted her into his arms like she wanted. He let his forehead rest against hers, needing that anchor. The darkness tried to take hold like it had all those years in hell, but he was stronger now.

Or at least he tried to be for Becca.

She was the one who pulled him out when he needed it. He just hoped he wouldn't rely solely on her to keep his wolf and inner demons in check.

With a nod to Liam and Alec, he walked back to his home—his mate in his arms. In actuality, it was more of *their* home at the moment. He knew that the kidnapping and subsequent threats had forced her to move faster than she'd liked, but he'd take what he could get. They were mated—a bond deeper than marriage—and were living together. They were slowly getting to know one another, but he knew they had a lot more to talk about.

As he set her down on her feet in their living room, Becca rolled her eyes. "You know, when I said 'in your arms' I didn't actually mean you had to carry me out of there."

Hunter shrugged. He liked having her in his arms. Why bother letting her walk around when he could carry her and keep her close. He trusted Liam and Alec to watch his back, so he didn't need to keep his arms free.

"You know the only reason I let you do that was so you didn't have to deal with Dorian's glare if I wanted down."

He furrowed his brows. "You wanted to get away from me?"

"Seriously? That's what you got out of that?" She tapped her foot, her lack of patience in his understanding of women evident.

"Explain what you mean then."

She threw her hands up in the air, though she still smiled. "I mean, oh alpha-man, that I can walk by myself. I'm not a damsel in distress." Her brows furrowed. "Okay, so I was once or twice since you've met me, but I'm trying not to be. I might like being in your arms, but you don't have to carry me around like a child. I only let you do that so Dorian wouldn't be an ass about it."

He loved the way her green eyes lit up when she was passionate about something, whether it be her opinion or when they were making love. Her hair bounced around her head, as if it were just as wild as she was.

Gods, he loved her.

"I love you, Becca."

Becca froze, and Hunter cursed himself. He knew she wasn't ready to hear that. She'd been human her whole life, and he knew she'd been hurt in the past. She hadn't told him how, but he had a feeling it was bad. He was a wolf, meaning when he found his mate and found things he liked about her, he fell in love.

Quick and hard.

"How...how...what did you say?" Her voice shook, and he swallowed hard.

Damn him and his impulses. He should have kept that feeling to himself until she was ready. The cat was out of the bag though, and he couldn't take it back, not without confusing and even hurting her.

"I love you, Becca mine. You don't have to say anything back, but I figured you'd like to know my feelings. This way there's no confusion as to how I feel about you."

"Hunter...I...I don't know what I feel. I mean, damn it, I like you so much. I like being with you. I want to be with you. We're mated, and I know that's forever, but the words? I don't know if I can say them. I mean, not yet. Hell, I sound like an idiot. I'm sorry."

Though the pain arching across his chest hurt like hell, he pulled her into his arms, inhaling her scent. He knew she loved him because she wouldn't have said yes to forever without feeling it. But saying the words that might never had been said to her in the first place beyond her friends and feeling those odd feelings were two different things.

"Take your time. I'm not going anywhere."

She nodded, wrapping her arms around his waist.

"I'm not good at this love stuff, Hunter. I mean, I never had it has a kid, you know?"

He didn't know since she'd never told him about her past in detail before, but he nodded anyway, letting her talk. He wanted to take in every piece of information he could get from her, even it was in small batches that he had to piece together later.

He pulled her to the couch, where she snuggled into his side as though she'd always been there.

She let out a breath then rolled her eyes. "I swear it's cliché. My dad left us when I was a baby. Apparently being a dad and husband, or boyfriend since I'm still not sure they were even married to begin with, was too much for him. That left me and my mom, and, well, Mom wasn't the most caring or interested mom out there."

Anger churned in his belly at the thought of her being left behind by the man who should have cherished and nurtured her. His parents might have died when he was younger, but before they had, he'd known they loved him. He had a feeling he wouldn't want to hear more about just how non-mom-like her mom was, but he sat silently, rubbing small circles on her back.

"It's not like she starved or beat me or anything. I know a lot of kids had worse. Mom never kept a job for long and had too many men in her life to count. She used to tell me that the only way to make it as a woman in this world was to be strong enough to know when to lean on a man for something." The last part came out laced with bitterness, and he didn't blame her. "We always had food on the table, sometimes it was meager, but it worked. The men though..." She swallowed hard and he pulled her close.

Rage clawed at him, his wolf pacing, but he held back, needing for her to finish her story before he went out and tore off heads.

"They never touched me, if that's what you're thinking."

"Tell me," he growled then swallowed hard to keep his wolf at bay.

"When I got to my teens and developed breasts, some of my mom's men started to pay more attention to me than her. She got pissed and slapped me a few times, but there wasn't anything I could do. It wasn't like I asked for it, you know? I was too young to leave anyway, and I wanted to finish school. Then, well, then Mom got a new guy who wanted to do more than just leer."

Hunter's grip tightened on her waist, but he didn't trust himself, so he didn't say anything.

"The dude got his hands on me, but I was quicker. I kneed him in the balls, and when I went to tell my mom what happened, she didn't believe me. She slapped me again and called me a whore. Then she kicked me out. I was seventeen at the time, so I was at least old enough to finish school and stay with friends. Then, when I graduated, well, there was nowhere else to go. Luckily I stumbled across a help wanted sign at Dante's."

It seemed he owed the dragon more than an apology.

Shit.

"Hunter?"

"I'm not going to ask for the name of the man who touched you because killing humans would lead us into trouble, however, I'm glad you got out of there when you did."

She nodded then kissed his jaw. "I'm glad too." She took a deep breath. "I...I love you too, Hunter."

He blinked. "Really?"

"Really, but don't let me freak out, okay?"

He nodded then pulled her closer. She wiggled so she sat on his lap, his cock directly over her heat.

His mouth found hers in a heartbeat, their tongues tangling, their teeth clashing. While before they'd started out soft and ended hard and fast, now he wanted her beneath him, over him, and his cock buried deep in her heat.

He stripped off her top then groaned as she pulled away to stand up and take off her pants. He followed suit then pulled her down over his cock. They both groaned at the sensation, her pussy tightening around him. He'd smelled her arousal, so he'd known she was wet before he'd entered her, but shit, next time he'd have to use a little more finesse.

"This is going to be quick, Becca. I don't think I can last long."

She smiled then froze. "Shit. A condom."

He blinked then gripped her hips to lift her off of him. It

would about kill him, but he had a feeling she wasn't ready for a child if that were to come about. They'd been sure to use condoms after their first time mating, but fuck, he'd miss the feel of him bare inside her heat.

She gripped his wrists, stalling him. He could have broken her hold a thousand times over, but her light touch alone would freeze him.

Anything for her.

"We'll use one next time," she whispered, and Hunter tried to tamp down the warmth in his chest. He was a wolf, a strong one at that. He couldn't be floored by the connection to a woman.

Fuck, okay, he could be.

Only for her.

"You know we don't share diseases, but Becca, we could make a baby. Are you okay with that?" His cock was still buried deep within her, so he couldn't believe he was actually formulating sentences at this point.

"I'm just ready to fall off that ledge and be with you fully."

He snorted then kissed her head. Oh, his Becca, not the most romantic of words, but he'd take them.

Hunter gripped her hips then flexed his pelvis up, slamming even deeper into her.

She slid her hands up his arms to hold his shoulders than threw her head back as she rode him. Her breasts bounced in front of his face, and he leaned forward to take one in his mouth. Hell, she tasted so sweet, like a drug he couldn't get enough of.

He let her set the pace, slow and sensual as she rocked against him then hard and fast. His balls tightened as sweat rolled down his back. He'd be damned if he came without her, so he slid his hand down to rub against her clit. The little nub swelled at his touch, and Becca let out a whimper.

His fingers played along her clit and then where they were joined before he finally felt that sweet, sweet fluttering of her pussy around his cock.

He came at the same time, his seed filling her up in long

spurts. Both out of breath, they leaned against each other, and he wrapped his arms around her waist.

Hell, he could get used to this.

"Love you," she whispered.

"Love you, my Becca."

****

Fury coursed through Jason's veins. He couldn't find his damned study partner, Becca, and it was killing him.

Okay.

Not literally but he'd kill her once he found her if he didn't find her soon.

"What the hell do you mean you can't find her?" Jason spat into the phone. He paced his office, knocking gold and bronze coins off his desk. He hated the damn things since they cluttered up his place, but since he had to count them daily before putting them in the vault, he dealt with them.

Being part of the leprechaun council wasn't for the weak-minded, but shit, he hated the paperwork.

And coins.

He hated coins.

They were everywhere.

"She hasn't been back to her place in over a month. Just that fucking dragon and a few of her weird friends to check up on the dump," his second-in-command answered on the other end of the line.

Jason pinched the bridge of his nose. This was fucking ridiculous. He needed to find Becca. He'd chosen her to be his for a reason. She was one of the seven lightning struck, meaning she had power running through her veins. He wasn't sure what she was or how he could use it, but he wanted that fucking power.

Plus there weren't enough women in his realm, and he could always use a good fuck. Becca was all wild and fiery, and he'd have fun fucking that out of her over time.

He just had to find the bitch first.

"I want her found, damn it. Don't call back unless you have the bitch in tow. Understand?"

"Sure, whatever you say, but why can't you just use one of the other women?"

"Because I want that one!" he screamed into the phone before pressing *End*. Fuck, he missed normal phones where he could slam the receiver down. Pressing *End* just wasn't the same.

Someone knocked on the door, and Jason took a deep breath. He couldn't kill whoever was on the other side for pissing him off.

Well, he *could*, but it was bad for business.

"What?" he spat.

"There's a wolf out here for you, sir," his secretary...uh he couldn't think of the little bastard's name, said.

"Why the fuck is there a wolf outside my door?"

"I'm not going to huff and puff if that's what you're afraid of," a tall man drawled as he pushed through the office, an annoying smirk on his face.

The other man radiated danger, causing Jason to almost take a step back before thinking better of it. "Who the fuck are you?"

"I'm Dorian Masterson, council member of the Nocturne Pack and your new best friend."

"And why are you my new best friend?"

"Because I have a leprechaun in my midst, and I had a feeling you'd want her."

"Her?" Jason's pulse sped up. There were only a handful of leprechaun women alive. Their race was slowly dying because they weren't allowed to mate outside the species, not that Jason would ever want to mate with a wolf or human anyway.

"Yes, her. I think you know her as well if my intel in correct. A certain lightning struck woman named Becca?"

Jason just about came in his jeans at the glee running through him. Becca? *His* Becca? A leprechaun. Fuck, this was the best news from fate he'd ever heard.

"She's a leprechaun? So I take it she found what her power was." He tried to keep his voice calm, but he knew the wolf had sensed his excitement.

"Yes. She found her true half in our Beta. Now that won't work for me."

Jason remembered the fucking wolf who'd dared to threaten him at Becca's place, and he snarled.

"Yes, I take it you know of Hunter. I want him dead, but I can't do it the normal way, so I'm going to do the next best thing."

"And what is that?"

"Take his mate away and force him to kill himself."

Jason smiled. And when they took her, they'd have a new Breeder. Because of the lack of women in their societies, they were forced to be with many men at a time, producing child after child until their bodies were eventually spent. The Breeders were a deep secret among the leprechauns. Women and some of the men had tried to rise up against the council for rights and privileges, so Jason had been part of the group to cull the herd. It was easier to rule with an iron fist then deal with naysayers.

Becca would become a Breeder and save their people...and he'd have her all to himself at night.

He might have to chain her up for a while, but she'd get used to it.

"What do you need from me?" Jason asked, his body hard with excitement.

Dorian smiled.

Oh yes, this was the beginning of a beautiful alliance.

Chapter Eleven

Life as a leprechaun wasn't all rainbows and gold coins. Okay, Becca thought, it wasn't really much different from her regular life. Sure, she felt a bit stronger and had more endurance—much to Hunter's delight—but she couldn't do much of anything else.

Apparently she might have some form of magic, but that hadn't shown up yet.

She also should have been able to transport her body from place to place, but it wasn't as if she knew how to do that. Getting struck by lightning and turned into another creature by her other half didn't come with an instruction manual.

Maybe she could convince Jamie to write one and sell it to anyone who went through this in the future.

Not that it would happen, but it couldn't hurt.

"What's going through that head of yours?" Hunter asked as he came up from behind her where they both stood in the kitchen.

He wrapped his arms around her waist and she instinctively leaned back into him. She'd never been a touchy-feely person before, but she couldn't help her deep need to be touched by this man. Maybe being surrounded by wolves had changed her tune. Everyone in the Pack was constantly hugging, kissing, and leaning into one another. Hunter had explained it was because wolves craved touch to feel centered and whole. She had a feeling some of it, though, was because wolves always seemed to be horny.

Okay, fine, she was horny as hell around Hunter, but still...

She'd already seen the effects of the moon on their hunts. Sure, wolves didn't have to turn on the full moon, but there was a crazed feeling on those nights. She'd stayed at home with Leslie on that night while Hunter went hunting with Liam and Alec. She still remembered the feel of the Pack, as if everyone was on edge and knew something glorious was coming. Most of the wolves hunted for prey. Liam and Alec had found a rabbit to eat while Hunter came home to her.

She blushed, remembering the knowing look on Leslie's face as she went back home. Hunter had taken Becca hard that night, as if his wolf was calling the shots. She didn't care about that though. She just cared that he'd made love to her with a fierce passion that had made her fall for the man.

Yes, she knew there was a difference between love and lust, but without the latter, the former would be boring. At least to her.

Plus he'd cared for her afterward, soothing every love bite and taking a long bath with her, as if he'd been aware he'd been rough. She'd liked it all, though, and had told him so.

She couldn't wait for the next full moon.

Hunter's lips trailed up her neck, and she turned to give him more access. She couldn't seem to get enough of this man—not like that was a bad thing.

They were actually talking about who they were beyond what fate had decreed for them. They'd also declared their love for one another—something she'd never thought she'd do.

This was a real relationship, not something that would fade with time.

At least she hoped not.

"You just sighed, Becca dear, but it wasn't a good sigh," Hunter whispered. "What's wrong?"

"It's nothing," she lied.

He bit her neck, and she gasped. "Don't lie to me, my mate. Tell me what's troubling you."

"Aren't you afraid we'll lose everything?" she blurted out. "This all happened so fast, and I don't want to rely on it too much."

He twisted her around so she could see the love in his gaze. "I'm always afraid someone will try to take you away from me. We're not safe, not yet, but I will *always* protect you. As for relying on it? I will always love you, Becca. You have to believe in that."

"I think I'm just feeling out of sorts."

"It's because you haven't set roots here yet, nor have you found your place in the human realm. I know you feel isolated out here, and I think, once we get through the meeting today, we can go back to the human realm and find a way to make both lives work. I don't want you to give up everything, and I'm not planning on forcing you. I'm also not planning on letting you go there alone, so you're going to have to find a way to make room for me in your life in both places."

A deep, fulfilling love filled her at his words. "You've been thinking about this."

"Of course I have. I might be dominating, but that doesn't mean I want to dominate you. We'll find a way to make it work in both places."

She let out a breath. "That means, I guess, we have to deal with the meeting first."

He nodded, his jaw clenched. "I'm sorry you have to deal with this, but it could be a good thing."

She raised a brow.

The leprechaun council had summoned her.

Summoned.

That couldn't be a good thing.

It wasn't as though they'd invited her to tea or something. No, they'd *demanded* her presence in front of their council that afternoon for some form of questioning.

So far, acceptance among her friends' new councils was fifty percent. Lily had been enveloped in the warm arms of the brownie world. They wanted to show her what it meant to be a brownie and told her she always had a home there. They'd even adopted Shade into their fold.

Jamie, on the other hand, had had a completely different experience. The djinn council at the time had *not* wanted Jamie. At. All. The old leader had wanted to kill Jamie for being an "abomination". He'd even struck up a deal with Balin's demon father, Pyro. Needless to say, that hadn't ended too well. The new djinn leader had a different approach and had cautiously warmed to Jamie, but Becca had a feeling it wouldn't be that easy. Even if Jamie forgave and forgot, her two mates wouldn't be so lenient.

Not that Becca blamed them.

After all, she'd almost died because of the old djinn leader. It wasn't as if she could just forget that feeling or the look on Hunter's face when she'd let out what she thought was her last breath.

She blinked as Hunter's lips captured her own, and then she sank into him. When he pulled back, she whimpered, needing more.

"That got the sadness out of your eyes," he whispered.

Was it any wonder she loved this wolf?

"I'm scared they'll reject me," she said.

He tucked a curl behind her ear then kissed her brow. "I can't predict what they will say, but know this, you will *always* have a place by my side and by your friends' sides. If the leprechauns act like idiots, you'll never be alone. If they do welcome you with open arms, well, it looks like we'll have three realms to deal with on a daily basis."

She grinned then kissed his jaw. He'd shaved for the occasion, but she still missed that soft rasp against her lips when he let his beard grow.

"Ready to go?" she asked, keeping her voice light.

"I'll go anywhere with you."

And that is why she loved this wolf. Just saying.

She looked down at her outfit and let out a little sigh. There really wasn't an etiquette for what to wear when one found out they were a new supernatural being and had to meet people like them...or at least like a part of them. She'd worn a cute sundress and shrug so she'd be covered but still look nice. Her legs were bare, but she wasn't showing too much skin.

Maybe she should have worn pants.

"Stop overthinking it," Hunter ordered as he pulled her toward the backyard.

Hunter's place was at the edge of the forest where they could still see the tall trees and sink into the darkness if needed, but there was some open space to run and enjoy the sunshine.

He held the summons in his hand that would, when ready, open a portal for them to enter the leprechaun realm. She still wasn't exactly sure how it all worked, but she was pretty sure most realms were locked to outsiders without special requests. The summons, which had arrived by mail of all things, acted like a connection between the two realms.

Becca didn't think she'd ever get used to how things worked now that they weren't human. At least she had a long time to learn more about it.

The portal opened in front of them, a swirling vortex of gold and green lights. She braced herself then took a step through with Hunter by her side. Cool tendrils of smoke wrapped around her arms and legs, pulling her through the stream until she found herself on the other end.

The forest was long gone.

No, now she stood at the end of the yellow brick road, or, at least, a demented version of that road. Large emerald buildings formed a city with zigzag streets paved with gold. There was an odd forest surrounding the city, with short squat trees.

The sky held her interest more than anything else though.

Rainbows.

Hundreds of rainbows.

They were woven into an interlocking web with strong bursts of light sparkles shooting through them as if someone was sending magic or messages through them.

Apparently the laws of physics and light didn't matter to leprechauns.

Good to know.

"It's like the *Wizard of Oz* on acid," she whispered.

Hunter snorted, and his frown remained. She knew he didn't like being alone without backup in a strange place, but the summons had strictly forbade it.

"What? No joking?" she tried keep her tone light, but it wasn't working.

"I don't know the area or the people."

"And we shouldn't antagonize. Got it." She squared her shoulders then took Hunter's hand.

As soon as she did that, a group of people stepped out of the closest building.

All were men.

All were redheaded.

Interesting.

The one in the front crossed his arms over his chest and glared at her before letting his gaze roam over her body. The others followed suit, and Becca resisted the urge to hide behind Hunter. They'd discussed before they'd left that she would do her best to stand on her own. She didn't want to appear fearful or weak in front of people she didn't know.

Not only would she have to find the courage not to run from people stronger than her—something she hadn't done in a while honestly—but Hunter would also have to swallow the urge to protect her at all costs.

The leering looks, however, creeped her out.

It was as if they didn't care she totally knew they were picturing her naked and other...things. She held back a shudder at the thought.

Gods, she just wanted to go home.

"The council is waiting for you both inside," the first man who had stared at her said.

She raised her chin and passed the group of men, Hunter by her side, and tried not to let any of them brush against her.

She couldn't be responsible for their safety if they acted on their thoughts with Hunter around. Hell, she had to hold herself back from slapping a few of them herself.

Where were all the women?

They walked into the large room with high walls and vaulted ceilings, and Becca knew this had been a mistake. She shouldn't have come. She should have just ignored the summons and stayed within the den walls with Hunter.

Yes, that would have been the cowardly way out and might have started a war, but hell, she had a bad feeling about this.

Okay, fine, she wouldn't have stayed away, but the thought was nice.

Five men sat on emerald-green chairs that looked to actually *be* made of emerald. Four of the men glared at her but didn't look any more dangerous than the men she'd passed.

The fifth, however, made her stop in her tracks.

"Jason."

He sneered at her, all semblance of the nice guy he'd tried to be before gone. Not that he'd ever been too nice before as he'd always creeped her the hell out. She'd only studied with him out of habit and her inability to say no. In his place was a man who leered at her like the rest.

"It's good to see you, my Becca."

"I'm not your Becca," she spat. Was nothing like it seemed? Her study partner who used to be bane of her existence was a leprechaun?

What else didn't she know?

"I see, Hunter, that you never told your so-called mate what I was," Jason teased.

Becca stiffened. That's right. Hunter had met Jason once before. He must have sniffed him our or something. Why hadn't he said anything?

Her mate leaned toward her, his lips brushing her ear. "I honestly forgot. He didn't mean much to me, and we've had other things to worry over."

She nodded, relief filling her. Hunter had told her when Dorian had tried to pry them apart. There was no reason not to trust him now. Jason had been a pest before. Now he seemed to be a pest with power.

Oh hell.

"Are you done mooning over each other so we can begin?" Jason asked.

Becca narrowed her eyes at the skinny little man who'd only annoyed her before. Now he pissed her off.

"Good," Jason said. "Congratulations on becoming something better than the little human you were."

Becca blinked. Seriously? What was it with other species thinking they were better than others? Sure, humans had their own issues with thinking they were better than other humans, but hell, why couldn't people just get over it?

"What is it you wanted?" she asked, sidestepping his taunt. She winced as she heard her own words. Not exactly the most gracious of things to say, but it had already been a long day, and things didn't look as though they'd get better any time soon. Sure, she'd wanted to act demure—okay, at least sociable— when meeting the people who apparently shared her genes on some basic level, but it didn't look like that was going to happen any time soon.

Jason glared for a bit then sat back on his chair, looking like a petulant child used to getting what he wanted. "Since you're now a leprechaun, you are under our rule. You're from a long line of glorious people who have fought wars and battles in order to gain our freedom. You might not have grown up within the leprechauns, but you are now one. You are part of us. You will obey us."

Becca blinked at Jason's convolved speech. An uneasy feeling spread through her, mixing with the anger, fear, and anxiety already crawling around in her belly.

"That means you get to stay here with us and become part of our culture. You're ours now, Becca."

"There's no way that's happening," Hunter growled, and

Becca agreed.

Jason raised a brow. "You, wolf, have no rights here. You were only allowed through our wards in the first place because you're mated to one of ours. That bond, however, will have to be severed. There's no way we'd let the likes of you into our fold."

"You can't do that," Becca said. True halves and mating bonds weren't something a person could change. That, at least, she knew for sure. If not, she'd been fighting the idea of it at first for no reason.

That, though, wasn't what made her heart hurt. Just the thought of losing Hunter made her want to scream...or do something.

He was *hers*.

No one had a right to take him from her.

"Oh, I wouldn't disagree with me, darling," Jason crooned. "When you join us, you'll be mine. A Breeder. You'll bear our young and enjoy the sensual pleasures of any man who wants you. Our culture is different from yours, so you'll have to get used to it. It's not something for the...faint of heart, but you'll like it. I promise. It's in your blood."

Revulsion slid through her.

Holy. Hell.

A Breeder?

No. Fucking. Way.

"We're done here," Hunter growled.

He took her hand and pulled her through the door. Becca looked back over her shoulder at Jason, who merely smirked at them. Oh, she had a feeling he might let her and Hunter leave the realm if they wanted, only to keep from inciting a war, but this wasn't the end of it.

Not by far.

Though some of the men stood in their way, the look on Hunter's face must have warned them away. The moved to the side, their arms still over their chests, their gazes still roaming her body, but they didn't stop them.

This, however, was only be beginning.

Hunter pulled his own portal, and they found themselves within the Pack's wards in another breath.

"Holy shit," she whispered.

Hunter pulled her into his arms, his body shaking. "I don't care what we have to do, you're *never* going back there."

She nodded then kissed him hard, needing to remind herself what was real and what was a threat. She had known it was going to be hard becoming something new, but she'd never thought it would be like this. They were monsters.

The others she'd met had been the nightmares that haunted dreams. They'd threatened and tried to scare her. Okay, they *had* scared her.

What the hell were they going to do?

Chapter Twelve

A week later Becca's arms were full with an adorable wolf pup, and her heart had settled. The little guy licked her chin, startling a giggle from her. Okay, so she sounded like a teenager, but come on.

Wolf. Pup.

This little dude was the definition of adorable.

"They make your heart just melt right down, don't they?" Leslie asked, holding a pup of her own.

The other woman had stopped by for their daily snack and gossip. Without Leslie, and even Liam and Alec, Becca wasn't sure she'd have made it stuck inside the den for so long. Between her change, the dangers from those who had taken her, the fact that she wanted to be near Hunter and get to know him, and the whole leprechaun thing, her time within the den walls kept increasing.

She missed her friends.

Hunter had offered to take her to the human realm so she could see them. He'd even offered to stay there for months. Becca, though, had put him off. She wanted to see her friends, but she knew Hunter needed to be here right now with the state the Pack was in, and Becca needed to be by Hunter's side.

She'd go back to her other home soon, even if it was just to remind herself that people liked her.

Though Becca had tried, she really hadn't melded with the rest of the Pack as much as she'd wanted to. People were still leery of an outsider and even more so of her because of what she'd turned into.

They'd never met another lightning-struck person before.

Sure, she'd met only her friends, but they didn't make her feel like a freak. Well, maybe Faith did, but that was only because her friend loved her. The other woman loved being snarky to her friends. That's how she showed her love.

The other members of the Pack, save a few, gave Hunter a wide berth also. Yeah, they came to him with their issues, and he hugged, cuddled, and helped them like a Beta was apparently supposed to do, but it wasn't the same.

Even an outsider like her could see the ambivalence the other members of the Pack felt about the wolf who had spent so much time fighting and killing in the demon games in the pits of hell. They didn't know what to make of him.

Hunter deserved more than cautious looks and bland smiles, but she didn't know how to help him. Honestly, she still didn't have a place for herself within the Pack, so it made no sense for her to try to make a place for him.

Today, however, she'd taken a step in joining the Pack in spirit, as well as body.

Today was babysitting day.

"I think I'm in love," Becca said as she nuzzled the five-year-old pup in her arms. He yipped then licked her chin again, causing another round of giggles.

"Brandon is a cutie, isn't he?" Leslie asked as Dylan, Brandon's twin, wiggled in her arms.

Apparently the twin boys' mother was a big *90210* fan.

"And they know it." Brandon pulled away from her to crouch low on the ground, his little butt wiggling in the air as he growled.

Becca rolled her eyes but tackled him like he wanted anyway. She was careful not to put any weight on him as he was just as careful not to let his claws out while he climbed all over her. Hunter had told her that pups were taught from their first shift, around age two, that they needed to keep their claws in while playing. Though wolf shifters healed quickly, that didn't mean children should rough each other up in wolf form. Plus, as babies and children, they loved wrestling with adults in human form, as Becca was doing now.

She wasn't sure if she healed as quickly as shifters, as she hadn't wanted to cut herself to see, but most leprechauns, according to Hunter, could heal slightly faster than humans, just not as quickly as wolves. From what she'd seen from her friends, Becca knew she'd get the full powers of the leprechauns, but that didn't mean she'd have them right now. Jamie and Lily had received all of their relative powers, just not right away, so maybe Becca would be the same.

That the den mothers trusted Becca enough to let her watch the twins—even with Leslie by her side—told her that some were trying to include her. She'd just have to try harder to make the next steps happen.

"When did you say Hunter would be home?" Leslie asked as she tickled Dylan.

Becca grinned despite herself. Simply hearing the man's name made her happy. She had it bad. "He said he'd be home soon." Actually, after he'd kissed the hell out of her and nipped along her neck leaving his mark for all to see, leaving her wanting and a bit dazed, he'd said soon.

That had been over an hour ago.

"He said he was going to meet with Liam and Alec, right?"

"Yeah, but I don't know about what exactly. It's not that he's secretive, it's just..." She couldn't articulate what she meant exactly. It was more that she figured Hunter was used to being on his own and not having to tell people where he was going and for what exact purpose. Becca didn't need to know everything either. There was a difference between knowing they'd be back and demanding to know everything.

"It's just that he's the Beta and has things to do," Leslie finished for her, and Becca nodded.

Brandon nudged her hand, and she felt a light warmth radiating *from* her palm. Becca spread out her fingers, letting the tingling sensation spread through her fingers. That had been happening a few times over the past week or so, but she didn't know what it meant exactly. To be careful, she pulled her hand back so she wouldn't hurt the pup.

Brandon shifted into his human form, leaving a naked little boy in the wolf's place. He quickly pulled on his clothes he'd left in the middle of the room then sat in front of her, his little brows scrunched up.

"What was that?" Brandon asked.

"I'm not sure. I think it's my powers." Well, she was pretty sure that had to be it, but she didn't want to make any rash judgments.

"Do you know what you can do yet?" Leslie asked, petting Dylan, who remained in his wolf form.

Becca shook her head. "I think I'm supposed to be able to heal. Eventually. Leprechauns, like other species, have different forms of magic. Since mine seems to be centered in my palms, Hunter thinks it has to do with healing. He also told me that I might need to find another leprechaun to help me figure out what to do."

Leslie frowned. "And that doesn't seem like a possibility."

That was an understatement. There was no way she'd risk asking someone she didn't know and end up in a Breeding program. She held back the shudder that came with that thought. "Nope. I might ask Ambrose, though, when I get back. He's old as hell, as I like to tease him, so he might know more than others."

"It's as good an idea as any."

A slight burn arched across her chest, and she gasped. Hot pain sliced along her mating bond with Hunter, and she cried out.

"Hunter."

"What is it?"

"Something's wrong. Oh sweet gods, it's the bond." She put her hand over her heart, trying to make the pain stop, but it only intensified.

Hunter was hurt.

Badly.

Leslie's eyes glowed, and she held out her arm toward Brandon. "I have the kids. Go."

Becca didn't know what good she'd be if Hunter was in trouble, but the bond pulsed, creating agony. Hunter needed her, even if she might not be so much help.

She needed him.

Gods, he had to be okay.

She threw on her shoes then slammed out the house, following the pull of the bond rather than a firm direction.

The smell of smoke hit her first, burning her nostrils, irritating her eyes.

Footsteps pounded on the ground behind her as others felt the fear in the air and caught sight of the tall, billowing column of black smoke coming from one of the older buildings in the den.

The same building where Hunter had been meeting Liam and Alec.

She staggered near where others were gathered, fear gripping her harder than the men who'd grabbed her from her apartment.

"Hunter!" she screamed as loud as she could. He had to be okay. She could still feel the bond, painful as it was.

That meant he had to be alive, right?

Movement from the front of the building caught her eye, and men and women ran to it, despite the fire. Others were getting fire hoses and buckets, trying to put it out. Becca ran toward the figure prone on the ground and gasped.

Her Hunter lay on his back, burns covering his body. Bad burns. She didn't know degrees, but she had a feeling they were threes.

"Hunter, oh gods." She fell to her knees at his side even as she saw Alec stumble out of the wreckage, Liam over his shoulders.

They were both burned from what she could tell, but not

as badly as Hunter. Others ran to their side, but she stayed by Hunter.

He raised a shaky arm, tucking a piece of her hair behind her ear. "Becca," he rasped out, low and sounding painful.

Warmth slid through her body, that oddly familiar tingling sensation wrapping around her palms. Instinctively, she placed her palms over the worst of Hunter's burns and watched as her hands glowed. Sweet pleasure, not the sexual kind, but the kind that made her feel of happiness, warmth, and promise filled her. Hunter's backed bowed as his eyes widened. She heard the murmurs and gasps of people around her, even over the roar of the fire and its eventual cleanup.

She was healing him.

His tissue and muscles knitted together in some places, the burns healing somewhat but not fully. She didn't know how she was doing it, only that she knew it had to be done.

She didn't know how long she kept at it, but as sweat slicked her back and down her temples, her vision started to blur.

"Becca, baby, stop. I'll live. You're hurting yourself."

She met his yellow gaze then let her arms fall to her side. For some reason her body felt really heavy and hard to move. Maybe she would just rest her head near Hunter's for a bit.

"Becca? Someone help!"

She heard her mate yell her name, but her eyelids were too heavy to look. She just needed a little breather, and then she'd be fine.

Hunter was okay.

That's all that mattered.

****

She was driving him crazy.

And not in the lust-filled, need-now kind of crazy Hunter usually liked from his mate.

No, this was the kind of crazy that came after years of

mating, not after a few weeks and an almost life-ending encounter.

The couch wasn't the place he wanted to be.

No, he wanted to run on four feet or two.

He didn't care.

"Becca, dear, stop hovering," he grumbled, but she just shook that head of hers, her pretty red curls dancing around her shoulders, then fluffed the pillow behind his back.

"How does that feel?" she asked, warmth mixing with the slight sternness he loved about her.

He leaned back into the pillows, noting that, yes, his back felt better and the burns on his chest weren't tugging as much anymore, but it was the principle of the thing. Becca was running herself ragged taking care of him. Sure, he was a little weak at the moment—he held back a growl at that—but he wasn't an invalid. He wanted to hold Becca by his side or rise over her as he sank his cock into that tight pussy of hers, but she was having none of that.

No, she wanted to make sure he was all healed and healthy before they did any type of cuddling.

Any type.

The wounds on his chest, though, weren't what that hurt the most. No, it was the memory of Becca's eyes rolling to the back of her head as she passed out along his side. He'd injured himself further by sitting up and pulling her into his arms, needing to see if she was okay.

She'd scared the shit out him.

He'd have gladly gone through life with scars and spent months recuperating from the wounds that would have killed a human than watch Becca go through what she did. Unsure of how to use her powers, she'd let them all run through her like an open faucet rather than siphoning off some of her powers at a time.

He hadn't known how to help her use her healing powers, and she'd almost died saving him.

He'd never let her do it again. No matter what. There was

no way he'd let her harm herself for him more than she already had. In fact, she'd already attempted countless times to heal his wounds further, but he refused.

"Hunter, why can't I just heal them a little more? I promise I won't pass out again." She bit her lip, her teeth sinking into that juicy piece of flesh.

The image went straight to his cock, and he couldn't hold back his groan.

"What's wrong? Are you hurt?" She ran her hands up and down his arms, and he had to find patience. Between those lips of hers and her hands on his body, he'd have to jerk off in the shower.

Again.

"I'm fine, Becca. I promise. And, no, you can't heal me. We already talked about this. Don't make me spank you."

Her eyes darkened, and the scent of her arousal hit him hard. He adjusted himself in his sweats, watching as her gaze latched onto his hand.

"Hunter Brooks, stop trying to turn me on."

He grinned despite himself. "You liked the idea of me spanking you, didn't you? I can't wait to see that little ass of yours all red from my hand."

She closed her eyes, and he knew she was holding back a moan.

"Should I leave the room?" Alec asked from behind her.

Becca's face turned that pretty pink Hunter loved so much, and he held back a laugh. "I think I've said worse things to shock your delicate sensibilities before, Alec."

His friend raised a brow in Becca's direction. "I would think it would be your mate's issue, not mine."

Becca fisted her hands on her hips then narrowed her eyes at Hunter. "You're just trying to change the subject. No, mate of mine, we are not having sex or spanking or doing anything dirty. Not until you are healed. That would come—and so would we—if you'd let me heal you."

Alec barked a laugh, and Hunter flipped him off. "You're

not healing me. Not until we talk to Ambrose about how to deal with your powers."

"We could go and talk to him sooner if you were healed." She grinned as she said it, and he knew his mate was just playing with him now.

"We're going around in circles, baby. I don't want you hurt." He said that last part in all seriousness.

"I don't like seeing you hurt *now*."

"I'm healing, baby. Liam is too. We'll be back to normal soon."

"Normal? What is normal? People being kidnapped and places being blown up? Sorry, that's not normal to me."

"Nor is it to me," Josiah said from the front door.

Hunter had felt his Alpha's presence a few minutes earlier, but Josiah hadn't walked into the house until just then.

Becca turned to Josiah, wringing her hands. His mate still hadn't gotten quite used to the overwhelming presence of the man before them.

"Oh, hi, Josiah. Can I get you something to drink?"

Hunter cracked a smile and darted a glance at Alec, who was doing the same.

Josiah gave her a sad smile then shook his head. "No, dear, I'm not thirsty, but thank you for your hospitality in your home. I know I'm an intruder, but we need to talk."

"You're never an intruder, Josiah. You're Hunter's family." Becca shrugged. "I guess that makes you my family as well."

Happiness filled Hunter at her words, and Josiah's expression brightened.

"That was the best thing you could have said to me today. Thank you. I am honored to be part of your family."

Their Alpha sank into an armchair while Becca sat on the end of the couch, keeping her hand on Hunter. Alec remained standing. Hunter had a feeling whatever Josiah had come over to say wasn't going to be good.

"Let it out, Josiah," Hunter said.

Their Alpha was starting to look haggard—something that scared the shit out of Hunter. They were in the middle of peace talks with four other Packs, something that Josiah had to deal with personally. That had to be keeping him up late at night. The fact that the Pack itself was fracturing within from those who desired power couldn't be helping.

"The three non-injured members of the council have summoned the Beta of the Pack."

Rage spiraled up his spine and sank into his muscles. "What the fuck? Why now? They couldn't kill me, so they've decided to bore me again in their chambers? Fuck them. I'm tired of this shit, Josiah. I know your grandfather created the council to ensure we didn't become like the other Packs who had a rampant need for power, but this isn't working."

Alec nodded. "Instead of creating a balance, it's allowed wolves, who can't become Alpha through tradition, to try any means to attain the dominance they crave."

"You think I don't know this?" Josiah exclaimed. "Of course I know what the other council members want. Without you and Liam, we'd have been fucked over long before this. The thing is, because we've had over a century for families to slowly gain ground for power, the Pack is in a state of flux. We can't just go in and knock heads around like we used to." A faraway look entered Josiah's eyes, and he cracked a smile. "Gods, I miss that."

"When do we need to meet in their chambers?" Hunter asked. He still resented the fact that the council had their own chambers while the Alpha and Beta dealt with the circle like they always had. Not that he wanted a chamber for himself, but he didn't like the fact the others had one when it wasn't needed.

"It's not in the chambers, son. They're calling a full circle. They don't believe you're strong enough to be Beta. Not with you being laid up and your... non-wolf mate."

Hunter took a deep breath, swallowing the anger, and took Becca's hand.

"Because of me? They don't think I'm good enough?"

Becca asked, her voice soft. "What does a full circle mean?"

Ignoring his wounds, he brought Becca up to his chest. He needed to feel her. She grounded him with her presence alone, her touch even more so. "It means that the council doesn't think I'm fit to be Beta."

"And I'm not fit to be your mate."

He clenched his jaw but nodded against the top of her head. "They want me to fight to remain in power."

"You can't do that. You're hurt."

The burns had weakened him, but it was the effects of the smoke inhalation and internal bleeding that he was worried about. He wasn't as fast as he usually was...wasn't as strong.

He didn't know what the outcome would be.

"I'll be fine."

From the look on his Alpha's face, Josiah saw the lies in his words, but it didn't matter. He'd fight.

He settled Becca off his lap and pulled himself up off the couch. He held back a wince and worse as his burns and internal damage screamed at him, but he needed to put on his warrior's face. He couldn't show weakness.

Not even to his Becca.

She stood and cupped his face. "You shouldn't have to fight. You already did your Beta circle thing. It's their fault you're hurt to begin with, though we can't prove it."

Hunter leaned and captured her lips, needing her softness and inner strength. "They can call me out if enough of the Pack believe in them."

She swallowed hard but nodded.

"I'm going," she declared. "You can't keep me away."

Though he'd rather she stay behind, he knew he couldn't hide her from the bad. She was Pack now.

Soon they found themselves to Liam's then to the gathering. They made their way to the Pack circle, Josiah leading the charge. Liam limped beside them, refusing to lean on Alec the way Hunter refused to lean against Becca. People had gathered again as they had for the circle he'd fought before.

It seemed like ages ago. Also like before, some looked as though they'd rather be elsewhere—either afraid of him or knowing this was all bullshit.

Dorian smirked as Hunter's group came through the edge of the circle. "Look at your Beta, Pack. He's weak."

Hunter growled. "Are you the one challenging me, Dorian? Step into the circle, and I'll tear your face off."

He was past all the political bullshit.

Dorian snorted. "I'm not challenging you, old man. You're not even the one we're challenging."

Something like fear slid through him. "Then why am I here?"

"We're challenging your mate. She's not strong enough to help lead the Pack."

"What the fuck are you doing?" Hunter yelled. "You can't challenge my mate."

"Oh, we don't want to take away the bond, since we can't anyway, but we can make sure our Pack is strong. We can't do that with *her* at your side or as part of the Pack."

Becca gripped his hand. Hard.

"Becca Quinn, the Pack challenges you for dominance. Lloyd's niece will be fighting you to reclaim our family's rightful place. Hunter, if your mate loses, so do you. Remember that."

"They can't do that, can they?" Becca whispered.

He couldn't speak. Couldn't move.

He couldn't lose her, but if he took her away from this, he left the Pack. His family.

It wasn't a choice though. Not really.

He turned toward Becca. "We'll leave," he whispered, words for only her ears. "I'll go lone wolf. We're done here."

She pulled away, her jaw set. "No."

Chapter Thirteen

Becca raised her chin. "You're not leaving the Pack. We can't let them win. I'll fight. I'll prove myself worthy." The Pack was out of their mind if they thought it was okay to rule like this.

They were fighting, killing, and breaking their rules in subtle—and some not-so-subtle—ways, and they were destroying their Pack from the inside out. Hunter was ready to leave the Pack that had raised him, the Pack that had been part of his blood for centuries, all because of her.

Okay, not solely because of her. She wasn't selfish enough to think that if she hadn't come things would have been different, but her presence wasn't helping. The council would have found another way to try to take down Hunter. They had a thorn up their ass about their Beta, and Becca was tired of it.

She'd be damned if she'd let her mate deal with this crap for the rest of his years. Something had to change, and if it took her fighting to prove her worth among a group of wolves who wanted her dead, then so be it. Dante and Shade had taught her to fight somewhat, and Hunter had taught her even more.

She wasn't completely helpless.

She wasn't a wolf either.

Her skin was just as fragile as a human's—weak and ready to bleed—but she was stronger than she had been before. As long as this Lloyd bitch didn't shift into her wolf form, Becca could probably battle her way through. Hell, why couldn't she have turned into a paranormal creature that was actually useful?

Like a tiger or something with sharp claws and pointy, pointy teeth.

Hunter cupped her face. "We're leaving." His tone held no call for disagreement, but she didn't care.

She turned to kiss his palm then moved back. "If we leave now, you're letting them win. You're letting the other Pack members who *do* believe in you fall into the hands of those who don't give a shit about them. If we leave now, I'm telling them that *I'm* not worth anything and not good enough to be your mate. I'm not letting that happen."

Hunter closed his eyes and took a deep breath, a strong shudder rolling over his body. The burn marks covering his chest looked as though they hurt like hell, and she knew his lungs and other internal organs weren't a hundred percent yet— something that could have been changed if he'd have let her heal him. That, though, wasn't something they could deal with at the moment.

"I can't lose you," he whispered, his voice so filled with pain that her heart broke for him.

"Don't count me out just yet. I need your strength."

And a miracle, but she wasn't going to say that out loud.

He closed his eyes, and she was afraid he'd say no. Or at least take her away from here before she could fight for them. She might have been stronger than she'd ever been, but she knew she was much weaker than Hunter, even if he was hurt.

And she wanted to fight a female wolf?

Hell, she had a death wish.

"The wolf you're fighting has a weak left knee. You kick her there, she'll go down, and then you can get her by the neck. This isn't to the death. You only have to pin her. As long as she's down on the ground and doesn't use her claws, you're strong enough to pin her."

Hope filled her, and she kissed his chin. "Thank you."

"Don't you fucking die, Becca. Do you hear me? If you die, I'll kill every wolf and creature who dared look at you funny then find a way into the afterlife and kick your ass for leaving me. Do you understand?"

She grinned at him, even though it was a bit forced. Gods, this was stupid, but if she didn't fight, she'd never prove herself to the wolves who didn't want a human—or at least a former human—in their ranks.

Hunter kissed her then, hard. She could taste the desperation on his lips, but it mixed with the determination to see her through his.

She could do this.

She had to.

"Are you two done pussyfooting around?" Dorian asked, boredom in his tone. "Anastasia is ready to fight. Let's get this over with."

Hunter kept his hand on her hip as they turned to face the circle again. The woman who Dorian had called Anastasia stood in the center, her fists on her hips.

Dear. Lord.

She looked like an Amazon. Or maybe a lean linebacker.

The woman had to be at least six three and all muscle.

No wonder Hunter was freaked the fuck out.

"Her knee, baby, her knee," Hunter whispered her in ear.

Becca rolled her shoulders back, unwilling to cower and show the fear coursing through her veins. This had to be one of the stupidest things she'd ever done, and that was saying something since one time she'd gone with Faith to a beauty school and had a bikini wax.

She held back a shudder at the memory of *that* experience.

Of course, with the way Anastasia glared at her, Becca was pretty sure she'd take another bikini wax over stepping foot into the circle.

"I don't see why I have to fight this little bitch," Anastasia spat. "She looks like a little whore, all saddled up next to one of our men. I could pick my teeth with her bones with a flick of my wrist. I don't even want that fucking Beta beside you. I'd rather pick my own man. Don't worry though, bitch, I'll take what I want, when I want. Why can't I find something worthy enough to challenge?"

Something? Well, wasn't this lady a peach. Not only had Becca just been called a whore, a bitch, and worthless, now she wasn't even a person? Oh, this just got better and better.

Becca gave one last squeeze to Hunter's hand then took a step into the circle. "You're name's really Anastasia? Seems like such a cute and pretty name for a big-ass butch of a woman like you."

Some of the crowd gasped, and she was pretty sure she heard Liam's chuckle.

Anastasia narrowed her eyes.

Good job, Becca, antagonize the woman who could probably break you in two with a sneeze.

"No claws or teeth," Hunter called out.

Relief washed over her at his words but didn't help with the tension she felt.

Just get the knee. Just the knee and she could pin the bitch down.

Maybe.

"Fine. I don't need to go wolf to kill this bitch." Anastasia smiled, and Becca had to swallow down the bile that rose in her throat.

Anastasia's smile wasn't so much a happy smile filled with rainbows and unicorns as it was more along the lines of "Yay, I get to play with my food before I eat it."

"No claws," Dorian agreed, as if he knew Becca would lose no matter what. Bastard. "This isn't to the death either, Anastasia."

The other woman pouted, actually pouted, at Dorian's words. Becca might have been grateful the guy had mentioned that, but she wouldn't put it past him to have an ulterior motive.

Maybe he thought being maimed and broken was better than death at the moment.

"Fine." Anastasia spat then moved.

And not just a normal movement, but *moved*.

Damn, the bitch was fast.

Becca ducked out of the way and rolled, but not fast enough. Anastasia got a hold of her ankle and tugged. Becca fell to the dirt on her back, hard, and tried to pull away, but the other woman was stronger. She might not have had her claws out, but the way she prowled over Becca's body reminded her of a caged animal.

Though she was aware of people around them, watching, cheering, crying, or worse, she ignored them all. If Lily and Jamie could get out of their own fights, then so could Becca. She scooted from beneath Anastasia and kneed the bitch in the chin for good measure.

Though her own knee hurt like a bitch from knocking the woman in the chin, Anastasia only spat out blood and moved closer. The wolf swiped out—sans claws—and Becca ducked again, this time using her shoulder to get Anastasia in the stomach. The other woman didn't move, but at least Becca was getting a few punches in. That had to count for something.

The other woman kicked and punched, hitting Becca more often than not, but Becca didn't back down. Pain radiated through her body, blood seeping from a cut on her lip. Her right eye started to get blurry, and she had a feeling she'd have one heck of a black eye come morning, but she didn't stop fighting. For every hit Anastasia got on her, Becca got one back.

She heard Hunter's anguished howl with every strike against her and shout at every strike on her opponent, and it spurred her on.

Throughout it all, she didn't forget her main goal.

The big bitch's knee.

But every time she tried to get a good shot, the other woman moved out of the way. Anastasia knew her own weakness and wasn't about to let Becca have a go at it.

Bitch.

The other woman punched Becca in the face, forcing her head to whip back. Though she didn't think any bones had broken, the blinding pain almost made her throw up.

The other woman smiled at this then laughed.

Her mistake.

Becca swallowed the pain—and the blood filling her mouth—and lunged toward Anastasia's knee. Caught unaware, the other woman howled in pain as Becca used her whole body to bend the wolf's knee all the way back. The sickening sound of tearing ligaments and most likely bone filled Becca's ear, but she didn't care.

Anastasia screamed and hit the ground.

Becca rolled then jumped on top of her, using her remaining strength to block the other woman's airway. Tears streamed down both their checks, but neither would yield. Anastasia tried to move under her, but Becca would have none of that.

She wasn't sure how much time had passed, but finally, on sweet gods finally, Anastasia slammed her hand down three times in the dirt, yielding.

Holy shit, the wolf didn't cheat.

She must have had more honor than Becca had thought.

A shocked silence filled the circle until cheers and growls rose among the observers.

Arms came around her, and she inhaled the heavenly scent of her mate, her Hunter.

"Becca, my Becca." He kissed the bruises on her face, but didn't let her go.

She'd won.

She'd fucking won.

How the hell had she accomplished that?

"This isn't over," Dorian spat.

Becca resisted the urge to punch the bastard in the face. Her body hurt too much for that.

"It's beyond over, Dorian. You've lost. Either back away and deal with it, or deal with me," Hunter growled.

"I guess I'm late to the show," another voice said beside them.

A tall, built man with long blond hair stood between

them, his face expressionless, his arms crossed over his chest. If Becca hadn't been in pain and in love with the man holding her, she would have thought this stranger was damn gorgeous.

This wasn't the best time to be thinking that however.

"What the fuck are you doing here, bear?" Dorian asked.

The other man—bear—raised a brow.

Hunter shook his head then placed Becca on her feet. "Jace, it's good to see you."

Hunter knew this man or bear or whatever. The guy, Jace, looked as big as a bear, so it fit.

"You called in a bear to come to our Pack?" Dorian yelled.

Jace snorted. "I'm a Mediator, you dumb fool, and it seems that the council should have called me in earlier."

What the hell was a Mediator, and why didn't Dorian look happy to see him? Well, that at least made Becca like the bear.

"Take me to the council chambers," Jace ordered, his voice holding no room for discussion. "I see we have a lot to discuss. Hunter, would you like to take your mate home to make sure she's healed?"

She answered for herself. "I'm fine." Hunter opened his mouth to argue, and she shushed him. "I'm not letting you go in there without me."

Jace quirked a smile, making him look even more handsome. "I like this mate of yours already."

"Hands off, Jace. Eyes too. Fine, Becca, you can come, but the minute it looks like you're going to pass out on me, you're going home."

She was fine, she knew it, but if Hunter wanted to freak out, she'd let him.

Jace raked his gaze over Hunter. "From the looks of it, you both look like you could use some rest."

"Tell me about it," Becca muttered.

Jace shook his head. "No, you tell *me* about it once we get to the chambers."

The other members of the council stalked toward the chambers. If they'd been wearing capes, Becca was sure they would have flourished them like Dracula with an attitude. It looked as though Jace was there to fix things.

That was good, right?

Once inside the council members, including Liam and Alec, took their seats. Josiah took his as well, with Hunter bringing Becca with him to the Beta's seat. Jace stood in the center, seemingly unconcerned he was below the rest of them in their tall chairs. After all, Jace was a big man. It would probably take a lot to intimate him.

"Who called you here?" Alistair asked, a little fear in his tone.

Though glad to hear his fear, Becca wasn't sure why the wolf looked so scared.

"Who called me here doesn't matter," Jace answered, his deep voice calm, but demanding attention and respect.

Becca saw the quick glance between Liam and Alec, and she was pretty sure who had done it. Good for them. They were in a no-win situation on the council as the only two level-headed men. The other three would win every vote just because they fought together rather than thinking on their own. Liam and Alec might have wanted to help the Beta and Alpha more, but with the rules and traditions as they were, nothing was happening—nothing *could* happen.

Hopefully Jace would find a way to help the situation. That is, if that was his job to begin with. She still didn't quite know what a Mediator was in respect to shifters. She could only hazard a guess as to his purpose.

"I'm here because your Pack needs help. I'm a Mediator, a shifter of outside council, sent to Packs, Prides, and other dens to ensure the fighting within the structure itself is settled."

"We know this," Dorian spat.

"I'm making sure Ms. Quinn understands," Jace explained. "I don't stop the fighting between Packs. It is up to you and your Alpha to ensure the Pack's safety, but I *am* here to make sure you guys don't kill each other over power. Or, if there is a struggle for power, to make sure you at least do it within your own rules."

Becca held back a snort—mostly because her face still hurt. Rules? Those were the things killing their Pack to begin with.

"Your rules and traditions, though, are the things killing you," Jace said.

She could really start to like this guy.

Hunter ran his hand over her side and kissed her neck, a proprietary gesture, but she loved it nonetheless.

"You think to come in here and tell us our rules are forfeit?" Lloyd growled. "You're nothing but a lone bear with too much power. You have no say here."

Jace growled, not a growl she was used to, like a wolf, but a terrifying bear growl that came from deep in his chest and practically shook the walls. She sank into Hunter's hold. At this point, she didn't care if she looked weaker than Jace for it.

She *was* weaker than Jace.

"I'm the Mediator. Watch your tone, old man. Your Pack is crumbling, and you need to do something about it. You all are fighting among yourselves so much that the blood of your weaker wolves is on your hands. What would happen if another den were to attack now? Would you be strong enough to fight them off? No. I don't think so. You're letting your pride fester into something tainted. I won't take the case yet because I want to see if you guys can handle it on your own without bloodshed. Now grow the fuck up and learn to run a Pack or I'll deal with them for you."

Becca blinked. Okay, so the Mediator wasn't some soothing, sweet-talking man but a bear who came in, could rough them up, and take care of things on his own.

Good to know.

"I'll be back soon to see what you've all decided but, for now, fix this shit."

With that, the bear stalked away, and Becca blinked. Hunter pulled her closer into his arms again despite his wounds and carried her out the chambers without another word. Liam and Alec followed behind with Josiah between them.

"What's going on?" Becca whispered, fear clawing at her.

"We have a few days, and then Jace will come in and decide for us who shall live or die."

"He can do that?" Gods, that was a lot of power and responsibility to put on someone's shoulders, as broad as they were.

"Yes, and he'll have to if we don't figure out a way to break the council. If everyone wants to live, the easiest way would be to disband it, but it's hard to go against tradition. It's even harder to do so when other Pack members seem to follow the three jackasses." He walked them into their home and closed the door. She assumed the others had gone home as well.

"You're going to break the council?"

Hunter nodded. "We're in a different time than we were when it was formed. It's not needed now and, really, is only a bunch of talking heads. We'd work better as an Alpha and Beta pair with enforcers, not a council."

She cupped his face, ignoring her aches and pains.

"How are you going to do that?"

He kissed her palm. "I don't know, baby, but we're running out of time to figure it out."

A shiver ran down her spine, and she nodded. If they didn't find a way to take down the unruly wolves, there would be nowhere to hide from a bear on a mission.

Of that, she was sure.

****

Jace Goodwin took a deep breath and closed his eyes, letting the human realm wash over him. Gods, he'd missed this place. He missed the hustle and bustle of humans and their problems. He loved the fact that he would never be called in to Mediate them; he only watched them from afar.

What he really missed, though, was the building he stood in front of. More importantly, he missed the *man* inside that building. He could already scent him, that spiciness mixed with dark chocolate and a hint of danger.

Gods, he'd missed that dragon.

He stepped through the front door and sighed with relief at the empty room. It would just be Dante and him, thank the gods.

It had been too long, and his bear needed his dragon.

Another scent, something far more delicate and sweet, brushed against him, and he froze. The scent faded away as quickly as it had come, and he frowned.

What was that?

Who was that?

"Where the fuck have you been?"

Jace smiled as Dante walked into the room from the back. That black with blue streaked hair of his had grown since Jace had last seen the man. His eyebrow piercing glinted in the overhead light, forcing Jace to remember exactly how many piercings the other man had and how much Jace had wanted to touch them all...but had never been allowed to.

"Is that any way to greet me?" Jace crooned.

"You were gone for years, man. Years. I tried to get a hold of you. Where the fuck were you?" Dante crossed his arms over his chest, a small tendril of smoke coming from his nostril.

Well, hell, the dragon was well and truly pissed. Not that Jace blamed him. He *had* been gone for far longer than he'd anticipated.

"I was stuck in the bird of prey area," Jace answered. "It took three years just to get through Mediations."

Though Jace had washed the blood from his hands, he wasn't sure he'd ever get the images of exactly what had gone on there out of his head.

Dante's posture relaxed slightly, but he didn't move closer. Jace didn't move either, unsure of his welcome. He hated feeling as though he was out of his depth, but that always came when he was near his dragon.

"I found her," Dante whispered, and Jace sucked in a

breath.

"Who...where...her?"

Dante grinned then walked toward him. Jace held still waiting to see what the other man did. At six foot eleven, there were only a few people around his height, and Dante, though three inches shorter, was one of them. Jace never felt quite so big and awkward around him.

Most days.

Dante cupped Jace's cheek, and Jace leaned into the touch. "I found her."

Jace swallowed hard. "What's she like?"

"You'll love her."

Oh, Jace had no doubt about that.

Dante frowned. "Why do you smell like wolves? And Becca and Hunter? What's going on?"

Jace blinked then cursed, moving back. "Fuck. I'm Meditating, or at least will be, for the Nocturne Pack. You know Becca and Hunter?"

Dante narrowed his eyes. "Becca is one of my best friends, and Hunter is her mate. Do I need to get her out of there for her safety? I've been letting her stay there to get familiar with her future, but I'll get her away if I need to."

Irrational jealousy at Dante's words filled Jace, but he shook them off. "I don't know what exactly is going on there, but I'll fix it. It's my job." One that on most days, he loathed. "That means, though, I can't put you and her in danger right now. As soon as I fix this, I can come back though. Come back and stay."

Something flickered over Dante's face before he blanked his expression. "We won't be waiting forever, Jace. You need to come home. Protect Becca and Hunter then come home."

He didn't have all the facts concerning the Nocturne Pack so he couldn't quite promise to protect Dante's friends. He wanted to do anything for this man, but he wasn't sure.

Jace nodded then ran a hand through Dante's long hair, unable to stop himself.

"I'll come back. I promise."

"Don't take years this time, Jace. Nadie doesn't have that kind of time."

Nadie.

He liked that name.

"I'll deal with this fast. I promise."

Pulling away so he didn't kiss the man and make a fool of himself by coming in his jeans, he walked out the bar, hope filling him even as a slight edge of annoyance fought against it. He needed to get through this Mediation, and then he could have his future.

Finally.

Chapter Fourteen

O h, hell, you have got to be kidding me," Becca mumbled to the little stick in her hand. The thing seemed to yell at her and curse her for her carelessness. Okay fine, it didn't yell but stared back with an oddly loud silence, but whatever.

The two pink lines mocked her, telling her that she should have used a condom. Should have used more thought, rather than wanting to feel Hunter buried between her legs, filling her up with his cum.

It wasn't as if, at the time, she'd forgotten how babies were made. After all, she'd been on top of Hunter with his cock firmly in her pussy at the time, so she *knew*. It wasn't as if she didn't want babies with her mate; it was more because of the whole danger thing.

The whole Pack-is-out-to-get-them thing.

She couldn't have chosen a worse time to be pregnant.

Becca swallowed hard at that word.

She couldn't be pregnant.

The lines mocked her again.

Fine. She *could*, but why did she have to be so damn fertile? It must be Hunter and that sperm of his. They must be like super sperm and on wolf steroids or something.

Oh gods. She was going to give birth to puppies.

She didn't even know how to take care of a real puppy, let alone a baby wolf.

Or would it be a leprechaun? Hell. She didn't know any of this. She didn't know what genes would win out or even if one would to begin with. For all she knew, none of the paranormal genes would win and she'd end up with a human baby. The whole idea that humans came about in the first place because different species, like wolves and leprechauns, kept procreating until finally there wasn't more than a small smidge of supernatural DNA left.

She didn't even know how to teleport yet. Sure, she'd learned to heal other people slightly, but Hunter hadn't let her do much more than a cut or scrape, afraid she'd pass out like she had before. She really was a waste of a leprechaun.

She wasn't even lucky in the slightest.

Images of Hunter holding a little pink-blanket-wrapped bundle filled her mind.

Tears spilled down her cheeks, and she sniffed. Okay, that would be lucky. Her sexy mate holding a little baby girl...or boy...and being all overprotective.

That she could get on board with.

She wasn't sure that could happen though. Not with the danger at the fringes of every aspect of her life. The council hadn't backed down truly, but at least it was quiet for the moment. It was as if they were as scared of what Jace might be forced to do as she and Hunter were. Jason and the other leprechauns hadn't come for her, but she had a feeling if they knew she was pregnant, things wouldn't be pretty.

Gods, she needed to talk to someone. As much as she loved Leslie, she wanted her old friends. It had been ages since she'd talked to any of them, and she felt adrift. She shouldn't have isolated herself. She couldn't even blame Hunter for it ether. Countless times he had told her he'd take her to the human realm and stay there as long as she needed, but she had sworn she'd be okay learning the Pack.

What she'd really done was hide from her past and try to immerse herself in a future she was so sure she might lose.

Gods. Why hadn't she seen that before? She'd been so sure she'd lose everything like she had when she was a kid that she'd refused to let Hunter go. But, in doing that, she'd let her friends go.

Well, fuck that.

She needed the girls to talk to.

Becca stood on shaky legs and placed her palm on her stomach. She was only a month along or so, not far at all, but there was a life growing inside her. A part of her and Hunter.

She was so fucking scared.

The need to get out of the den and go back to where she'd come from clawed at her. It wasn't as if she wanted to be gone forever, but she needed a moment or two away from all the dangers and fears clutching at her so she could figure out how she really felt about a baby.

Right now her mind seemed to be going around in circles, which wasn't helping anything.

Quickly, before she could change her mind, she put on boots and put her hair in a ponytail. She just needed to breathe. She put the positive test in her purse so she could keep it close then walked out to the living room where Hunter was reading through old texts. He'd been trying to find a peaceful way to get rid of the council, and she knew he was coming up empty.

"I need to leave."

Hunter's head shot up. "What?"

"I have to go. I can't stay here anymore."

Shock, then sadness, spread over his face before he slowly stood up and stalked toward her. "You said you'd never leave me. I told you I wouldn't let you go."

Despite the fact she knew she didn't want to leave forever, everything that had happened over the past few months just spewed over her. "I need to go. Now. Just let me see my friends. You can't keep me here, Hunter." Gods. What the hell was wrong with her? She *knew* he hadn't forced her to stay here, but right now, at this moment, she needed air.

He raked a hand through his hair. "I never said you had to stay here, Becca. You could have gone and seen your friends whenever you wanted. Why are you acting like this now?"

"Are you saying I can't go?"

"No, baby, you can go. I'll take you now to see your friends, but tell me you're coming back with me."

At the word baby, she flinched. Hunter caught the flinch, his face turning to stone. He bend forward so the only thing she could see was his gaze. "I'm never letting you go, Becca. You're mine as much as I am yours. I will take you to see Faith and the others, but I'm bringing you back to where you belong. By my side. Then we can figure out a way to live in both places. I promise."

She didn't say anything, unable to voice what was going on in her head. Yes. She wanted to be by his side, but in doing that, it was too much. She just needed a break from the danger, and she needed her friends.

Becca swallowed hard, and Hunter searched her face before stalking toward the door. "Let's go."

She followed, knowing she'd done something she might not be able to fix. Her head hurt too much to figure it out but she would.

She had to.

The portal opened near Faith's house, and they stopped in her backyard. Hunter pulled her into his arms and kissed her. Hard.

"You're mine, Becca. I'll never keep you in a cage, but don't run from me. I'm staying in this realm. I have my phone. Call me when you want to go home."

Home.

Yes, the den was her home. She just needed to be in a place that wasn't constantly trying to kill her.

"Becca?" Faith called out from her porch. Hunter waved to the other woman than stalked away, going who knows where, leaving Becca clutching her purse. Nadie running out from behind Faith.

"What's wrong?" Nadie asked as she hugged her close.

"I'm pregnant," Becca blurted out then started to sob.

"I'll kill him," Faith said later as she set a pot of tea on the coffee table. "I'd have brought out the tequila, but since you're knocked up, that didn't seem like the best thing to do."

As soon as Becca had blurted out her condition, Nadie had pulled her into Faith's house and onto the couch, holding her close. Faith had mumbled something about stupid pricks and condoms then went to get the tea.

Becca still didn't know why she was overreacting or why she hadn't told Hunter. Gods, she felt like an idiot. It wasn't as if she thought Hunter would take it badly. Quite the opposite in fact. He'd probably puff out his chest and walk around as though his little soldiers had done something truly heroic. Then he'd wrap her in bubble wrap and try to keep the big bad wolf from blowing their house down.

It was that whole big bad wolf thing that Becca didn't think he'd be able to control.

It wasn't as though she didn't think Hunter or Josiah were strong enough. It was that they'd have to go against their Pack and their traditions to make things happen.

How the hell had her mind made its way back to the war brewing with the den?

"Okay, you need to tell us exactly what happened," Faith demanded. "I need to know if you want me to castrate the bastard or not."

"Faith, stop trying to take vital body parts off of Becca's mate," Nadie admonished then turned to Becca, who still lay against her. "But I'll hold the bastard down for Faith if you need me to."

Becca snorted out a laugh—exactly what she'd needed. "I've missed you guys so freaking much."

Nadie squeezed her close while Faith rolled her eyes, but Becca didn't miss the happiness in them.

"If you missed us so much, you shouldn't have stayed in the freaking den for so long," Faith said. "I mean, come on, one minute you're dating the man, the next you're kidnapped, saved, and living with him with stars in your eyes. Not that I knew there were stars in your eyes because I hadn't actually seen you. For all I know, things have been perfectly dreadful, and yet, you haven't come to us."

"Hell, make me feel like a bug beneath your shoe, why don't you?" Becca whispered.

"We just missed you, that's all," Nadie soothed.

"I'm sorry I stayed away for so long."

"No you're not," Faith corrected. "Yeah, you're sorry you couldn't see us, but from that bun in your oven, I'm pretty sure you enjoyed most of your time."

Becca laughed then told them about what had happened in the den while she lived there. She tried to make the parts with Hunter and how much she loved the man the most important parts, but her friends were more interested in the fact that she was now a leprechaun with either a death threat or Breeder threat hanging over her head.

"Why the fuck didn't we know about this?" Faith yelled as she paced her living room.

"Faith."

"No, don't start, Becca," Nadie said, albeit calmer than Faith. "Dante said only that you were being taken care of and happy. He didn't mention that people were still trying to kill you or that the realm that was supposed to welcome you with open arms seems to have turned into a crazy bunch of wackos that only want you for your uterus. He knew about all of this, didn't he?"

The betrayal laced within Nadie's voice made Becca feel about two inches tall. Damn it. What had she been thinking? Why had she stayed away from her friends for so long just because she wanted to see her future?

"Nadie, hon, he didn't know everything. I'm an idiot. I tried so hard to examine what I wanted my future to be, even if I didn't know it exactly, that I threw my past away or at least hid it."

Faith plunked herself down beside Becca. "I'll forgive you in a bit because I sort of understand."

Surprised, Becca turned toward her friend. "You do?"

Faith sighed. "Yeah. I do. I mean, you're still not off the hook for ditching us, and even more so in trouble because you haven't explained how good Hunter is in the sack yet, but I'll get over it."

"Faith!" Nadie blushed, and Becca just laughed.

"Tell me why you understand because I don't know if I do."

"You love him, Becca," Faith said simply. "All of this is so new, so of course you're going to be confused. Come on, it isn't like you had the most stable of childhoods, and, hell, even your twenties sucked a bit with doing so much at once and not taking any of the help we offered."

"Faith."

Her friend held up her hand. "No, let me finish. You're our best friend. We seven have been through hell, and for some of us that means literally. We've been struck by freaking lightning and now look at our future. Of course you're going to want to see what the other side looks like and immerse yourself in it. You're too afraid that if you step away from Hunter for even a little bit he'll leave like everyone else did—excluding your friends—and you'll be alone."

Becca swallowed hard. Though that had been what she'd been thinking, it still hurt to hear it. Gods, she was an idiot.

"I think I need to learn to multitask a bit better."

Faith snorted. "Honey, every time you multitask you end up dropping things. It's okay to need to compartmentalize a bit. Just, next time, make sure you don't take that so close to heart."

Nadie rubbed her hand on Becca's shoulder. "Why are you here now, Becca?"

Because she was an idiot, and she told that to her friends. "Besides that? Because I...hell. I guess I got scared. Hunter is freaking amazing. Even when he's all tough-alpha-wolf dude, he's always putting me first."

"Maybe you just wanted to test him," Faith put in.

"That makes me sound like a bitch. It might be true, or I

just got scared. I hate those women who throw fits just to test their men. I've never done it before, and I'll be damned if I let this end here."

"You'll explain it to him in a bit," Faith said. "Ambrose texted saying your mate is hanging with him and Balin at their place doing manly stuff."

"Ambrose didn't say manly stuff," Nadie said. "And Ambrose actually texted?"

Becca snorted, trying to imagine the five-thousand-year-old angel texting.

Faith smiled. "Jamie is forcing him to learn new things. As for the manly part, I might have added that, but it doesn't make it untrue. Your Hunter will be by to pick you up in a bit. Despite what you're thinking, he understands. Well, not the pregnancy part, but the fear-of-everything part. When are you going to tell him you're having his puppies by the way?"

"Wolves don't have litters, so I don't think I'll be having like eight babies at once," Becca teased, feeling better by just seeing her friends. "And I'm going to tell him we're having a baby as soon as we get back home. I'm not hiding this, and knowing his nose, I can't hide it for much longer anyway. I only got the pregnancy test to begin with because Leslie, another wolf, snuck it to me and I hadn't wanted to worry Hunter more than he already is."

Faith nodded, and the three of them started to talk about what she'd missed while she'd been away. These two women, and the other women who were part of their inner circle, were, or had been, her anchor. Hunter might have become that now, but her friends would always be there as well.

She just needed to remember that.

Chapter Fifteen

Hunter stuck his hands in his jeans pockets and stared at the back door to Faith's place. He felt as though he'd just left Becca there, yet at the same time, it felt like it had been years. Gods, he missed her more than anything, and his wolf, just like the man, needed to know she was safe.

The moon glared at him, as if it knew he'd somehow fucked it all up. Not even the night air and freedom that came from being away from the den could help him right now.

Hell, he didn't know what to do. He didn't know if Becca would be ready to go home or not.

He didn't even know if she still considered the den home.

Fuck.

What the hell had he done to scare her away?

Ambrose and Balin had told him that something must have happened to trigger her freak-out. Throughout everything, Becca had been strong and resilient.

Something must have changed, but he had no clue what.

"Hunter?"

Becca's voice broke him away from his thoughts, and his eyes shot open. He hadn't even been aware they'd been closed. Without second-guessing himself—at least for now—he strode toward her and lifted his mate into his arms. He buried his nose against her neck, needing to take in her scent to calm his wolf, to calm himself.

It wasn't that she'd been out of his sight; no, he wasn't as crazy as that. It was because they'd left each other on uncertain terms—something he'd rather not do again.

Ever.

He'd find a way to make everything better for her, make sure this worked. He wasn't about to let her walk out of his life.

She was his.

Forever.

Her arms wrapped around his waist and held on tight. His body relaxed against her, loving the way her body sank into his.

He could scent the other two women near them, but they'd stayed in the house, watching over their friend. Hopefully Becca had confided in them so she wouldn't have to bear it all on her shoulders, though he'd have preferred if she'd talked to him as well.

After a few more minutes of just holding each other and letting their bond settle over them, he pulled back and framed her face with his hands.

"Are you ready to go home?" He fought to keep his voice even and unassuming. He didn't know what he'd do if she said she wanted to stay with Faith or go back to her old apartment.

Alone.

If she'd wanted to go back to her old place with him by her side, he'd do it in a heartbeat. Liam and Alec could take care of his duties for a little while. After all, that was what he'd wanted to do in the first place when he was deciding how to have him fit within Becca's life as much as she'd given up things to fit within his life. He'd even told her that, but now he wasn't sure if she understood or even believed him.

Hell, he wanted, no, needed, to make sure that whatever happened now wouldn't ruin everything for the future. If only she'd talk to him.

He had no idea when he'd turned into a man who needed to talk and vent his feelings, but at this point, he'd get over it. He might have grown up within a Pack that prided itself on the fact that they weren't human and didn't abide by all their human laws, but right now, he needed Becca.

It wasn't like before she'd come into his life in that alleyway. Before he could have just walked to any female's dwelling and gotten his rocks off if he wanted. No, now was all about Becca. Other Pack members might have been okay with random, hardcore fucks whenever they wanted, but he needed the woman in his arms.

He needed to kill anyone who harmed her. The three council members' lives were forfeit. Or at least they would be soon. Hunter would have to deal with the fallout later from breaking the oaths and sanctions of the Pack. Those men had tried to kill his mate, his future.

It was past the time of words and prayers. Now he'd have to deal with the actions of others and the consequences of his own.

The leprechauns were also on his list. They might have been quiet for now, but Hunter had a feeling it wasn't over. No, not by a long shot. For all he knew, they were planning something right now and ready to catch him and Becca unawares.

That was not something he would let happen.

He looked down at his mate and fought to keep the warring emotions and thoughts off his face.

"Are you ready to go home?" he repeated.

"Yes. I'm ready."

Her soft words slid through him, and he almost fell to his knees.

Thank the gods.

He wasn't ready to let her go. No. Scratch that. He'd *never* be ready to let her go, and she'd just have to learn that. He was a dominant wolf, and he couldn't let go of the one who was meant for him by fate, biology, heart, and so much more.

She'd just have to get used to it and tell him why she'd reacted that way in the first place.

Right now, though, he just wanted to get her home, behind the walls of their home, in their bed, and under him.

His wolf needed to reaffirm the bond.

The man was right there behind his wolf.

Hunter gave a nod to the two women in the window then opened a portal to take Becca and him home. Thankfully Faith had a full coverage of trees in her backyard, so it made things easy. If they hadn't been in such a hurry in the first place, he would have brought Becca here on his bike. He loved the way she laughed when he went faster and hugged him tight, her body pressed against him, her pussy hot against his back with just the little amount of clothes they wore between them.

Becca slid her small hand in his, and he relaxed even more.

It never failed to floor him how her touch could make him react.

There was no way he was letting that go.

No way was he letting her leave him.

No way was he letting her keep whatever was bugging her away from him.

They stepped foot in their own backyard as the portal closed behind them. Night had fallen when he'd been at the triad's home, and it was even darker within the den, as the tall trees blocked some of the moonlight.

He smelled the smoke from someone's fireplace, and he could hear the gentle sounds of his Pack members relaxing for an evening. He kept Becca close as he used his senses to see if there were any intruders or anything out of place, but he didn't catch anything.

It seemed Liam and Alec had done as they'd said and watched over his home, as well as the Pack. Hunter could still smell the faint traces of the duo as they'd run over his land, keeping outsiders, if there had been any to begin with, away.

"Ready to go in?" he asked and looked down at his mate.

She tilted her head up and gave him a small smile, but he could still see the sadness in it. It broke him that he didn't know why she was acting this way, why she'd needed space.

They'd have to talk about it soon because there was no way this could go on, not even for a full night. He was too wired to protect and care for those he loved to stand idly by and let things fall apart.

He'd already had to do that when he'd been in hell.

There was no way he'd do it again.

They walked inside, shucked their shoes and her purse, and then walked into the living room.

"Tell me what upset you, Becca," he said as soon as they were both on the couch, her tucked under his arm.

Right where she was supposed to be.

She took a deep breath and leaned against his shoulder. His wolf paced, loving the way she felt against him but needing to know what exactly was going on.

"I think it was just everything."

"Everything." Shit. What did that mean?

"I mean, gods, Hunter. Everything that has happened lately is freaking terrifying if you look at it all together. We met because I was mugged and almost raped in an alley."

He clenched his jaw, forcing back the rage at that memory.

"I almost died when that piece of wood sliced through me as the djinn attacked."

This time the rage mixed with the horror at what had happened. If it hadn't been for Jamie's wish...

She moved so they could look at each other's faces. He tried to school his features to avoid scaring her, but he didn't think he was doing a good job.

"I can still remember the way you howled. At the time it was like an echo, so far away, but something I could still hold on to. I know Jamie's wish is what saved me, but if you hadn't been there on the other side, pulling me through..." She shuddered. "You were the one for me then, even if we didn't know exactly what to do about it."

He tucked a lock of her hair behind her ear then traced his finger down her cheek. He didn't speak, knowing she needed to let her words out and find a place.

"Then, when we finally became a couple, or at least were

trying to, considering my own pig-headed human way, the council changed all of that. Ever since, things have been crazy, Hunter. It's like it's one thing after another, trying to test us or break us apart."

He frowned, knowing she was right, but still not liking the words. He hadn't done enough to protect her from his own past. He knew that, but it didn't make it any easier to swallow.

"I'm sorry I'm not a better protector," he whispered. "I should be stronger than I am, and yet, you keep getting hurt."

She shook her head quickly then framed his face with her hands. He placed one of his own on top of hers, needing the touch.

"It's not your fault the world is out to get us. Okay, maybe not the world, but enough people with ego trips that it feels like the whole world. You're doing all you can, and I know you want to do more. You can't without endangering others, Hunter. I know that."

"It's why you needed to leave though."

She shook her head again. "No, maybe, I don't know. I think it was all too much, and I just needed to breathe again. I hid away here from my own past and decisions, leaving my friends worrying about me. That was selfish."

He frowned. "They knew where you were and how things where. You weren't selfish."

"I feel like that now, and from now on, I'm not going to be. I'm going to have to find a way to blend both worlds."

He nodded. "Done. I'll help. Anything you need."

"You're just what I need, Hunter. I hope you know that."

She smiled, though he felt as though there was something else he was missing. He kissed her forehead, needing to touch her again, and stiffened.

There was something different about her scent. Something...sweeter...softer.

His eyes widened and he dropped his jaw.

"Holy shit. You're pregnant."

She pulled back, her eyes wide, but not full of the surprise he'd have expected.

"You knew."

She winced. "I found out this morning. I think that's what caused the whole freak-out. Not that I don't want this baby, because, oh gods, I do, but because everything is going so quickly."

He blinked, his mouth opening and closing. He wanted to say something, but he hadn't the words.

Pregnant.

His mate was pregnant with his child.

An image of Becca large and round, naked with her hair covering her full breasts and her hands resting on the place where she grew their future filled his mind, and he smiled.

"We're having a baby," he whispered.

A baby.

"Hunter? Are you okay?"

He nodded slowly, everything like words and actions taking a bit longer to process than usual.

He was going to be a father. Becca, a mother.

Holy shit. This changed everything.

He pulled back so he could place his hand on her flat stomach. "I...I..." He had no idea what he was trying to say, but whatever it was, apparently his brain had gone on meltdown. A happy meltdown, but one nonetheless.

Would she freak out if he ran around the yard and howled to the moon so everyone would know that he gotten her pregnant?

Too alpha male?

Probably.

"You're pregnant."

"You said that already. Are you okay? What are you thinking?" Becca's words sped up as she talked, as if she were afraid of what he might say, how he might react.

"I'm..." He stood up and brought her with him, needing to feel as much of her as he could. "We're having a baby. I'm so fucking happy right now I want to strut around and tell everyone how male I am because I got you pregnant."

She snorted, laughter dancing in her eyes. "I can totally picture you doing that. In fact, I think Shade did that exact thing when he told us Lily was pregnant."

Hunter grinned at the thought. "It looks like our baby will have a playmate."

Becca gave a small smile then full-out and threw her arms around his neck. "We're having a baby!"

He lifted her off her feet and spun her around, unable to believe his joy. "Wait." He froze and set her down. "I shouldn't be twirling you around like that. You should rest or lie down or something. Should I bring you tea? No. You can't have caffeine. I think I read something about no milk either. Or maybe that was lots of milk. Hell, I'm going to have to go read some baby books right now so I know what to do."

Becca threw her head back and laughed. "We can learn together, though I think we're going to need to see the Pack doctor instead of a human one. They'll tell us what to do and what to read. As for twirling? I think that's okay. I mean, come on, you don't expect me to sit around and do nothing strenuous this whole time, do you?"

He had considered doing just that, but the tone of Becca's words told him that would be a bad idea.

"Hunter, if I can't move around, we can't make love. Get it?"

He froze then nodded slowly. "Oh, yeah, I don't want to quit doing that until the last possible minute."

She grinned. "So we're okay? I mean, after what happened earlier?"

He nodded. "We're perfect. As for why you freaked out before, we're handling that. Right now, though, I want to shut out the rest of the world and make love to my mate."

She bit her lip and looked up at him through lowered lashes. "I thought you'd never ask." Then she bent down in front of him and traced his dick through his jeans.

He swallowed hard but didn't move. "Becca, darling, what

are you doing?"

She looked up at him then, and he about came in his jeans at the sight of her kneeling before him, her hand on his crotch and her wide eyes looking up at him. Oh, hell yeah, he couldn't wait to fuck her mouth.

"I thought I'd give you a present for being so understanding," she teased.

He ran a hand through her hair. "Any time you want to put my cock between those lips of yours, all you have to do is ask. You don't need a reason to suck me off, baby."

She quickly undid his jeans and took his dick out. Just her touch made him want to blow, but he had more control than that.

At least a little.

She licked around the crown and then underneath to the sensitive area that made his eyes roll to the back of his head. He forced his gaze on her then wrapped her hair around his fist and pulled a bit.

Her eyes widened as she looked up at him, her pupils dilated with need.

"You want to go slow tonight? Or hard and fast?"

She kissed the tip of his dick then smiled. "I think when I get too pregnant, we'll have to be creative and a bit softer, and when the baby comes, we'll have to be quieter. So why not go all out and have you fuck me hard while you can?"

He groaned and tugged on her hair so she was looking directly at him again. "I'm taking all the control tonight, baby. My wolf is on edge, and I need you."

"Anything," she whispered.

He pushed her head toward his cock, and her mouth opened. He wouldn't force her to choke on him, but he wanted her to know he was the one in control and yet also know that he would never hurt her.

She swallowed the head of his cock, moving her tongue as she did so. He pulled her back by her hair, leaving a wet trail on his dick.

"Lick down my dick then suck on my balls. I want to be nice and hard for you when I come down that pretty throat of yours."

She looked up at him, pure pleasure on her face. "You're pretty hard right now."

He didn't grin, but he wanted to. "I'm going to have to punish you for that sass a bit later."

She grinned and didn't look too worried about her punishment.

Good.

His mate licked and sucked along his length until she reached his balls. She pressed his cock up to his stomach so she could get better access then started sucking. She started on one, letting it roll in her mouth then letting go with a pop, before licking over to the other one and repeating the process. He tapped on her hand covering his dick, and she let go, knowing what he wanted. He held his dick himself as one of her hands gripped his thigh, the other one reaching around his balls to rub his perineum. He groaned and loosened the grip on her hair so she could have better access. Her finger rubbed hard then moved back to circle his hole.

They'd never done finger play on him before, only her, but if she wanted to explore, fuck, he'd let her.

As long as she knew whom exactly was in control.

She pulled back and slid her hands in her jeans then slid them back out, her fingers slick with her own juices.

"What are you doing, baby?" he asked gruffly. Oh, he knew *exactly* was she was doing since they didn't have lube in the living room, but he wanted to hear her say the words.

"I want to play," she teased.

"You going to fuck my ass with those fingers of yours?"

Her eyes widened at the vulgarity then nodded.

"Can you do that with my dick in your mouth?" he asked. He had a feeling as soon as she started rubbing his prostate he'd come hard, and he'd rather it be down her throat than on her face and tits.

"I think so."

He grinned then pulled her closer. "Suck," he demanded.

She took him into her mouth, sliding along his length then pulling back. He let her set the pace while she was learning, but he'd take over soon.

She was still fully dressed, and he wore his shirt and his pants were down around his knees.

So. Fucking. Hot.

He felt her fingers around his hole testing, teasing, and he clenched his jaw. Finally, she pressed one slick finger against the opening and slid it in. They both froze at the sensation for a moment before she started working him. He gripped her hair hard so her head remained still.

"I'm going to fuck your mouth, baby. That way you can focus on what you're doing back there, okay?"

She nodded with his dick in her mouth, and he held back a smile.

Fuck, his mate was hot.

He pumped his hips slowly, letting her catch up. She widened her jaw to take more of him, that slick heat almost as good as her pussy. Her finger worked in and out of him as he moved, but she also ran small circles over the bundle of nerves, and he had to hold back from coming right there.

He wanted to let the pleasure ride out a bit before he came.

He fucked her mouth hard, pulled back when he hit the back of her throat, and then set a decent pace that left them both panting and sweat-slick. Finally, that tingle at the base of his spine shot up, and his balls tightened. She pressed down on that bundle of nerves, and he jetted down her throat. He gripped her hair and forced her head to stay close to his body so she could swallow him all.

Finally, he moved back, and she licked her lips and brought her hands down to her lap.

Damn did they make a pretty picture.

"Did you like that, my Becca?"

"Gods yes, can we do that again?"

He grinned down at her then picked her up by her shoulders until she was pressed against him. "Any time you want, but right now, I'm going to take care of you. However, I think I owe you a punishment for that sass of yours and for you leaving me before."

Her eyes widened, but not with fear.

"Go into the bedroom, take off your clothes and kneel on the bed on all fours."

"Okay."

Thank the gods, Becca was all in.

She scurried away, but not without swaying her hips just so for him. His cock filled again, and it was as though he hadn't just exploded a minute or so ago.

He stripped out of his clothes and tossed them on the couch. He had to force himself not to go in the bedroom right away and get started. No, he wanted to take his time and ensure Becca was ready for him.

After a few more minutes, he walked naked into the bedroom and sucked in a breath at the sight before him.

Becca knelt on all fours on the bed at the edge of the bed, her head lowered, her ass and pussy facing him.

She was perfect.

"I'll never hurt you, Becca," he whispered as he walked toward her.

"I know."

"I'll just use my hand. I know you like that little sting, but not too much, and I love seeing your ass red from my hand."

A shiver ran over her body, and he smiled.

Oh yes, she was ready.

He slid his hands up her spine, loving the soft feel of her skin beneath his palms. She shuddered under his touch, and he inhaled her scent.

He pulled back so he could get a good look at her ass and swallowed a groan. Hell, he had the most beautiful and sexy mate alive.

Her ass was plump and ready for his hand. Her pussy was wet, ready for his lips, his tongue, his fingers, his cock...him.

He couldn't wait to pound into her and feel her pussy clamp around his dick like a vise.

First, though, he had things to do.

He rubbed his hand along her pale ass, the softness creamy. He leaned down to kiss the small of her back, and she groaned.

"This is for that sass of yours," he growled softly.

His hand came down hard on her ass, and she gasped then let out a little moan. He was sure not to hit too hard but just enough to give them both a little sting. He slapped her four more times on one cheek then five on the other, making sure to never hit her in the same exact spot twice.

He stopped and looked down at his work. Her ass was a fine pink, blushed and stung from his slaps.

Fuck, she was gorgeous.

"This is for leaving me," he said.

He spanked her again, this time slightly harder, but she just threw her head back and moaned at his touch. He counted to five on each cheek, and then when she looked as though she was ready to fall onto the bed, spent, he slapped her pussy.

She gasped and looked over her shoulder, her eyes wide, full of need.

"Did you like that, my mate?"

"Yeah. Hell, I didn't think I would, but yeah."

He grinned, feeling cocky as hell. "Good." He slapped her pussy four more times, but not as hard as he'd slapped her ass.

She came on the last slap, a blush rolling over her body as her limbs shook.

He hadn't even entered her with his fingers or cock, and she'd come.

"You're so fucking beautiful when you come, baby," he said as he walked to the side of the bed so he could look at her.

He leaned down and captured her lips, aware he'd been remiss in tasting his mate.

"I love you," she whispered as he pulled away.

"I love you too. Now back up on all fours. I'm going to bury my face in that pussy of yours, and then I'm going to fuck you hard."

She shuddered again, and he smiled, pleased at her reaction. "Anything you want."

He went back to his position at the end of the bed and buried his face in her pussy, just like he'd said he was going to do. Her sweet juices coated his tongue, and he lapped them all up. He gripped her ass and spread her cheeks wide, getting better access.

He fucked her with his mouth then bit down on her clit. She came again, hard.

While she was still in the throes of her orgasm, he stood up and thrust into her heat. They both froze, the action full, heady.

She looked over her shoulder and panted. "Fuck me."

He smiled then pulled out before ramming back in. He gripped her hips hard, and he knew he'd probably leave bruises, but they'd be his mark, and she'd love them. He pounded into her over and over again until he felt his balls tighten, but he didn't want to come without seeing her face.

He quickly pulled out and flipped her over so she was on her back. She bounced slightly, and even before she hit the bed again, he was in her, fucking her for all they were worth.

Sounds of sweat-slicked flesh slapping together mixed with their moans and pants. He reached up and tangled his fingers with hers as their gazes met.

They came together, hard, and on a wave of sensation that surpassed anything he'd ever felt before. He groaned her name then found her shoulder and sank his fangs into her flesh again, needing to mark her.

He felt her mouth on his shoulder and knew she'd done the same, drawing blood, yet making her his.

Hunter pulled away and looked down at the mate in his arms who carried their future within her womb and smiled.

This was it. This was all he needed.

He'd be damned if anyone tried to take it from him.

He'd kill them all.

Slowly.

****

Dorian ran a hand through his hair and cursed. It wasn't supposed to be like this. The fucking Beta was supposed to be long dead, but no, he had to come back from hell with vengeance on his mind.

They were running out of time to make their plans work.

The Pack wasn't on his side anymore, not like they had been before when he and his men were spreading rumors about the weakness of their Beta and his choice of mate.

Things would have to change now if their plans had any hope of working.

Alistair and Lloyd stood off to the side, their age and weariness seeping off them like an oily stench that reeked of desperation.

Dorian couldn't wait to get rid of them once Hunter was dead and there were easy avenues to Josiah's throat.

Jason, the leprechaun douche bag that Dorian had to deal with, finally entered the abandoned building where they said they'd meet thirty minutes ago.

"Where the fuck were you?" Dorian spat. "You're fucking late, and I don't take kindly to disrespect."

The other man blanched but didn't apologize. "I'm here. What's the plan?"

Dorian narrowed his eyes. He'd deal with this bastard later as well.

Hunter and that bitch first, then everyone else.

"You got onto our lands before to set that fire, and no one saw, so I know our earlier plan worked," Dorian said.

Jason grimaced. "But that bastard is still alive. Who would have thought that tasty cunt was a healer."

"I don't fucking care about that anymore. It's in the past, and we have new plans. You're going to come onto our lands again and take Becca. It doesn't matter if people see you because I'll make it seem like it was Hunter's idea all along. That he wanted to get rid of his mate."

Yeah, not so much. Dorian was going to put all the blame on Jason's shoulders, but the other man didn't have to know that.

"And what about when Hunter comes to take Becca back? You might protect me from the Pack, but what about that fucking Beta?"

Dorian shrugged, secretly pleased Jason was falling for it. "Kill him. Use your men. I don't fucking care. Just kill them both or fuck her then kill her. I don't care. Just keep them away from the den while I... I mean *we*," he added with a glance toward his other council members, "take over the Pack."

"Tomorrow?" Jason asked.

Dorian grinned. "Tomorrow."

Then finally, fucking finally, all would be his, and that bastard Hunter would be dead.

Finally.

Chapter Sixteen

Everything was going to be okay, Becca thought as she put the last of the laundry away. Doing mundane tasks like laundry and cleaning helped keep her mind off the fact that things were totally not okay right now. Hunter was even cooking more when he was home to make sure she was fed and healthy, and she knew it was another way he was trying to make things normal.

They weren't normal though.

It had been only three days since she'd found out she was pregnant, and everything had changed.

She wasn't fighting for herself or even for Hunter anymore. She was fighting for a little baby who hadn't even come into this world yet and was completely helpless.

There was no way she'd let Dorian and the others win.

No freaking way.

Hunter was in the backyard after having just come back from Liam's where he, Alec and Liam had a meeting. She was pretty sure that any day now something big was going to happen and Hunter would have to change the way the Pack was run forever.

Heady stuff.

As she stepped onto the back deck, wind brushed against her neck, and she looked up to smile at her mate. Hunter turned and grinned at her.

She opened her mouth to say hello then froze, and Hunter stiffened.

Tingles shot up Becca's spine as strong arms wrapped around her arms, pinning them to her body. She tried to move, but whoever was behind her was stronger.

A portal opened behind them, and whoever had her fell back, taking her with him.

She couldn't hear Hunter's words but saw him scream her name, running to her as fast as he could.

It would be too late.

The portal crashed down around them—something that had never happened to her before, and she hit the ground hard. Instinctively, she put her hand over her stomach, praying the baby was okay after being jostled like that.

She looked up into the sky and held back a sob.

Rainbows.

The leprechauns had taken her.

Becca stood quickly, ready to fight, and choked back a scream at what she saw.

At least fifty men stood around her in a circle. Jason stood in the center with her.

"Hello, my love. So glad you could join us. I'm so happy the portal worked. I would have just teleported, but I can't do that carrying a load. You know how it is. Oh wait, you're weak, so you have no idea."

"You...you took me from my home."

Gods, she had to sound stronger than that. She *was* stronger than that.

Jason strolled toward her, his stride entirely too cocky. "Yes. I took you from the den, but that's not your home anymore."

"Fuck you."

He slapped her, the sting forcing her to close her eyes for a moment before she faced him again. "*This* is your home, Becca darling. I told you before that you are a female leprechaun and, therefore, fall under the jurisdiction of our laws. You will be a Breeder. It's a privilege to spread those pretty legs of yours and bear our young. Don't you understand? You can save our people."

Gods, this dude was really full of it. Forcing their women to Breed with them over and over again wasn't the answer.

Not that she knew the answer to the lack of females in their population. Maybe the little double X chromosomes didn't want to be part of a world where they would be nothing but a uterus.

"I'm not staying here, Jason."

"You think your little wolf can save you?" He threw back his head and laughed. "Sweet girl, nothing can save you. We closed the portal permanently on our way through, hence the bumpy ride. Of course, even if he did make it through, he'd have to deal with my men here, and, well...I wouldn't want to place bets, but I don't think they'd be on hell's animal."

Becca winced at the nickname some had given Hunter when he'd returned from hell.

"He'll find me, and did you forget? I can save myself. I've done it before."

Once. With Hunter's help.

Jason didn't need to know that.

Jason slapped her again, and this time she tasted blood. She reached out to hit him back, but he gripped her wrist hard enough to leave bruises and threw her to the ground.

"I like it when you're feisty. I'm going to really like putting my seed in you."

She blanched as she thought of the baby already in her womb.

What would Jason do when he found out about that?

There was no way she'd wait long enough to find out.

Why couldn't she use her powers to teleport now? Why couldn't she find a way to get home?

"How...how did you find me?" she asked because something felt off. "How did you get through the wards and onto the den?"

"Silly girl, wards aren't strong enough for teleporting."

"You teleported?"

He smiled. "Yes, through the portal, so I could bring you with me. All I had to do was think of what I wanted most, and there I was, my arms wrapped around you like how they will be for the rest of our days."

That's what she had to do? Think of what she wanted most in the world?

That was easy.

Her baby's safety.

How would that help though?

Her body shimmered, and she felt herself moving, not sure how she was doing it.

"Fuck!" Jason screamed.

She moved through something similar to a portal, all shimmery and full of gold and green light, then screamed as she slammed into something solid though she couldn't see it. She fell to the ground hard, her body quaking.

"You think you can just leave me?" Jason spat. "I put locks on our portals, you bitch. You can't teleport without my permission. You're stuck here until I'm done with you, and by then, your poor little wolf will be dead."

She narrowed her eyes, her body still aching from whatever Jason had done. "How do you know that?"

"Do you really think I'm in this alone? How the fuck do you think I got in to the den so quietly both times?"

"Both times?"

"Who do you think started the fire, sweetie?"

Oh gods, Jason and the council were in on this together. Hunter was in danger.

There had to be a way to make Jason let her go so she could go back to Hunter and warn him that things were happening.

Wait.

Jason's magic couldn't work if he were dead.

Right?

She rose on shaky legs and screamed, lashing out with her arms. He covered his face, but not before she raked her fingernails down his cheek. He screamed, and she punched him in the gut then kicked him in the nuts.

There was no way she'd let her baby and mate die because this piece of shit had delusions of grandeur.

She kicked and punched and screamed, surprised the others didn't do anything to help Jason out. Maybe watching their leader get kicked in the ass by a girl kept them from helping the bastard.

Whatever.

Something sliver glinted in the light on Jason's waist, and she reached for the hilt and grabbed it.

Without thinking about the consequences, she plunged the knife into the heart of the man who used to study with her and had turned into a monster.

Jason screamed, a thin trail of blood seeping from his lips.

"Becca." Cough. "I only wanted our future together."

Her legs gave out and she sat on the ground beside Jason. Becca pulled the knife out and stabbed again. "My future is with Hunter, you bastard."

The light went out of Jason's eyes, and she choked on a sob as she stood up on even shakier legs. She held the knife covered in their leader's blood and faced the men.

"Let me go. I'm not one of you. I want nothing to do with this."

One of the men shrugged then blinked. "I don't really give a fuck what you do. Jason's magic is gone, so you can leave. Come back, leave, whatever. We don't want you. Your blood isn't pure enough for us. We have better Breeders."

Relief filled her at his callous words, and she thought of nothing but Hunter, trying to remember how she'd somewhat teleported before.

Her body shimmered, and she didn't even bother to give one last look at the man who'd tried to kill her.

He didn't matter.

Hunter did.

Becca landed in the den, not in the backyard like she'd thought, but in the Pack's circle and by Hunter's side.

Dorian, Alistair, and Lloyd surrounded him, but no one else was around to witness what was going on.

It looked as though she'd shown up just in time.

****

"Becca," Hunter rasped out when she showed up out of nowhere by his side.

It seemed she had learned how to teleport.

The front of her shirt and arms were covered in blood, but it didn't look like hers, and she held a bloody knife. Soon he'd want an explanation, but right now, he had other things to deal with.

Namely the three council members who wanted him dead.

Now.

He gripped Becca's hand then faced Dorian and the others. As soon as the portal had closed around Becca, he'd tried to break through. Though the realm hadn't had an invitation, he could have found a way through, but he had a feeling the leprechauns had used some form of magic to block his entrance.

Dorian had shown up soon after, along with the other two of the bastard's inner council, and a handful of other wolves, forcing Hunter to the circle. Hunter could have fought, but he might not have won against the twelve wolves behind Dorian at the time—not when his mate was in another realm, most likely fighting for her life.

The other wolves had left the council alone with Hunter so they wouldn't have to bear witness to the crimes about to happen.

Cowards.

"Why are you doing this, Dorian?"

Dorian snarled. "You think it's easy to sit back and watch my pack stuck in an archaic system? I want us to live and rule.

With an Alpha and Beta, we're nothing."

"It's not archaic," Hunter countered. At least not *all* of it was archaic. "It's the way we are wired. We're wolves. Not humans."

Dorian snorted. "Yet we mingle and blend in with them, trying to hide what we are. Yes. I know it's for the greater good, but what are we doing to ourselves? We're becoming useless creatures who don't understand the breadth of our powers. We follow an Alpha who uses words rather than strength to lead us. What use is that in war? What use is that when we can kill him?"

Alistair, the one who had always seemed to want to fight another way, held up his hands. "Now, now. We don't want any more violence than we have."

Dorian barked out a laugh and threw out his arms. "Look at us. We've provided the backdrop for violence and chaos, old man. You helped me send the fucker to hell because you thought it was for the greater good. If that isn't violent, I don't know what the fuck is. Don't pretend that all we've done is for the greatness of the whole."

Hunter growled at receiving confirmation of who had sent him to hell. Oh, he'd known this whole time, but to hear the words was another matter. "No, you did it for the power and authority over a pack that needs leadership, not crazy schemes and lost causes. We're crumbling, Dorian, and you're letting it happen. I'm just as much to blame in that respect. I've let our own rivalries and laws get in the way of what I should have done in the first place."

Josiah came out from the shadows, anger on his face. "The council is the reason our pack is fracturing. As Alpha, I lead by example. Not by words alone. We aren't the dark and depraved animals you so desperately want to annihilate. You've become the very creature you're afraid of. Our Beta is the one who should connect with the members individually, learn their needs and heal when he can. He hasn't been able to do that because you crazy fools want to kill him."

"You can't prove any of that," Lloyd spat.

Hunter's jaw dropped. "You just told us all, you fucking idiot."

"We didn't tell you about Samuel though," Lloyd said, and Dorian growled.

Becca squeezed Hunter's hand, and he grounded himself, his wolf snarling but waiting for the right moment to kill.

Dorian rolled his yes. "Fine. You'll die soon anyway, though I'd rather have had that bastard Jason do it. Samuel died because he was weak. He wasn't worth the shit we threw him in when we killed him. You weren't supposed to come back from hell. We bargained for their protection and help in our takeover, yet you lived and came back, so they obviously went back on their word. Fucking demons."

Hunter blinked. The depth of the council's betrayal ran so deep he wasn't sure he could even comprehend all of it.

Josiah came to stand beside Becca and Hunter. It would be a three-on-three fight since he had no fucking clue where Liam and Alec were.

"If you're looking for your two butt buddies, they're...indisposed."

Fuck. He'd just have to hope they were okay because he had other things to deal with. He looked at Becca quickly. "I can't protect you."

She looked up then kissed him for all he was worth. "I can protect myself. Kill him."

With those words of pure badass from his mate, he lunged. Alistair lunged toward Josiah, the idea of nonviolence seemingly forgotten. The two men fought, Josiah much stronger, but Alistair fought with the last of his courage and life.

Hunter sliced his hands along Dorian's shoulder. The other wolf jerked and reached out to do the same to Hunter.

He looked out of the corner of his eye as Becca rolled to duck a punch from Lloyd. Rage filled him, but he couldn't take his attention off Dorian, or all would be lost. Becca moved toward Josiah, and the Alpha covered her as they fought off the other two wolves together.

Good.

Hunter, the one with the most personal stake in Dorian, went back to his fight. They punched, kicked, and clawed for what felt like hours, but must have only been twenty minutes.

Hunter snapped Dorian's arm, and the other wolf screamed.

He pulled back as Dorian clawed Hunter in the stomach with his other hand. Pain shocked his system, but he fought on. They lashed out at each other, each strike just as painful and deadly as the last.

Again, from the corner of his eye, he saw Lloyd try to claw at Becca, and Hunter lost it. He reached out and, with all his strength, clawed Dorian through the chest, gripping the bastard's beating heart, and pulled.

The man's eyes widened for a moment, as if he couldn't believe what had just happened, then fell to his knees.

With the other wolf's still-harm heart in his hands, Hunter leapt toward Lloyd and clawed through his neck. Lloyd sputtered then fell to the ground.

Josiah broke Alistair's neck, and the battle was done.

Hunter dropped Dorian's heart and pulled Becca into his arms.

"Oh gods, Hunter. Are you okay?" She tried to pull away to look at his wounds, but he wouldn't loosen his hold.

"The baby?" he rasped out. "Are you and the baby okay?"

She lifted to her toes and kissed his jaw. "Yes. I think so. Oh God, Hunter. I love you so much."

"I love you more than anything in the world, my Becca. I never want to see you fight like that again."

She beamed. "I kind of kicked ass though."

Hunter growled. "Never. Again."

"I'm going to find Liam and Alec," Josiah interrupted. "Take care of your mate."

Hunter nodded toward his Alpha, the man who had raised him into the man he was and protected the Pack the best way he knew how.

He'd forever be grateful for the way the man had taken care of Becca when Hunter could not.

"Let's go home," Becca said. "We can worry about everything else in the morning. I just want to get this grime and gods know what else off me and go home."

Hunter kissed her. Hard. "As you wish."

Chapter Seventeen

Oh, right there, baby. Right. Freaking. There."
Hunter snorted at her words, and Becca turned over.
"You, my Becca, sound like you're about to come just from my hands on your back."

She smiled at him then gripped his dick, which just happened to be on her chest since they were both naked and he'd been straddling her to give her a well-needed massage.

He let out a groan then shifted his hips so he fucked her hand a bit.

"Looks like you're about to come with just my hand on your cock."

He grinned then moved off her. She immediately felt cold at the loss.

"Where are you going?"

He just smiled and took out the lube from the nightstand drawer. "I do believe I promised you a present for being all strong and badass during the fight two days ago."

A shiver ran through her, and she sat up. Ever since they'd started playing more in bed, she'd wanted to start to do more with Hunter. Yes, she'd done anal before, but never with him. Never when she'd been so connected on a magical and personal level with a man that it would mean more than just something taboo.

"Turn over," he ordered, and she shuddered.

She loved when he want all alpha and dominant on her. She trusted him to take care of her, no matter what, so it didn't matter that he ordered her to do things in bed. She'd gladly do them as long as she could touch the love of her life.

"Get on all fours. I'm going to fuck that sweet little ass of yours and make you come that way."

"You going to fill me up?" she asked, knowing he loved it when she talked dirty.

He groaned then slapped her ass.

Hard.

Who knew she was so kinky?

The cold lube shocked her for a moment before he rubbed it around her hole, warming it up. He worked her with one then two then three fingers, each time the sensation slightly painful but easing to a sweet bliss. She felt so freaking full just with his fingers. She couldn't wait to feel his meaty cock filling her up.

Hunter removed his fingers, and she whimpered. She felt his hands grip her hips, and she moved back, seeking him out.

"Don't move, baby," he said then swatted her.

She froze, waiting for him. The head of his cock probed her, and she moaned.

"Just like we practiced, baby. Relax and push back, and I'll slide right in."

She did as he said, and slowly, oh so slowly, he slid in until his thighs were flush with her ass.

"Oh gods, I feel so full."

"You're as tight as a fucking vise. Shit, this feels good. You okay, Becca?"

She nodded, the sensations almost too much. "Just fuck me. Please."

He pulled out slowly then back in just as slowly, waiting for her to really get used to him. After the third stroke, he increased his pace until he was fucking her hard. She gripped the sheets and rolled her hips to meet him, loving the way he moved with her.

"Fuck, I'm going to come. Touch your clit and come with me, baby. I'll hold you up."

She smiled at the need in his voice and rubbed her

swollen, slick clit until she came. He shouted her name and came with her. She could feel his dick pulsate within her as he jetted his seed, and she grinned.

Hell yeah. She loved this man.

Hunter pulled out, and she collapsed on the bed. He ran his hands over her and kissed her softly. "Let me clean us up, and then we can start our day."

"Best. Wakeup. Ever."

He smiled, kissed her again, and then strode naked to the bathroom.

Yep. She loved that man.

After they'd cleaned up and eaten, they headed out to the council chambers to meet Jace. Well, they really weren't called the council chambers anymore considering the council had been disbanded. After three of the members had been killed because of treachery, attempted murder, murder, and so much more, the council was no more. Instead, Liam and Alec would be lead enforcers, and their family lines would be the ones to help protect and rule, along with Josiah and Hunter.

That was how it had been ages ago, and Becca hoped that it would help the future of the Pack. After all, since she'd mated Hunter and become a leprechaun, she had a long future to look forward to.

As for the leprechauns, well, like Jamie and the djinn, Becca didn't think she'd be hanging out with that group any time soon. They'd sent a note with an emissary trying to say no hard feelings, but really?

Not so much.

Once the baby was born, and she was a little more settled, she was planning on figuring out a way to change things for the women in that realm, but she had a feeling it would be a long time coming. At least she'd have a goal and job now, something much different than opening a bar because it was the only thing she knew how to do.

Oh she still might do that, but it wasn't as though she had to decide now. She had tons of time to figure it all out. Right now, though, all she wanted to do was be with her mate, her baby, and her friends—new and old.

Liam and Alec met them at the door to the chambers and hugged her. She loved that duo. They were like brothers and would totally be great uncles for her and Hunter's baby.

If the guys would ever figure out that they were totally in love with each other, it might even make things easier down the road.

That, though, was another matter altogether.

They walked into the room as a unified front, and she smiled as she saw Jace there. With that long blond hair and fantastic build, he was totally hot.

Hunter growled, and she held back a chuckle.

Jace might have been hot, but the only growly man for her was the wolf by her side.

She leaned into her mate's side, and he wrapped his arm around her as if proclaiming to the world whom she belonged to. Well, as long as he belonged to her as well, it was okay with her.

The bear gave them a crooked grin. "Glad to see you guys handled this without me." He sobered at his words.

"I'm glad you didn't have to make those decisions," Hunter said. "Does that mean you're done here?"

Jace shrugged. "I'm done with your Pack unless you need me as a friend. I think, though, with that mate by your side, you'll be fine."

"Are you leaving to go home, or wherever you come from, then?" Becca asked.

The bear grinned. "No, I'll be around for a long while."

With that cryptic comment, he changed the subject, and they discussed exactly what they would do with the Pack. All of Dorian's followers would either be exiled or demoted in rank. They would have to prove to the Pack that they were loyal. The ones in the Pack who hadn't taken sides were already showing their loyalty, and some had even bowed to her, declaring their protection and faith in her.

It seemed they'd been just as afraid of Dorian as she had

been and hadn't wanted to get hurt. While Becca understood that and had hugged and smiled with the ones who were afraid, she'd never forget the ones who had stood by her side in the first place.

She placed her hand on her stomach and smiled. She had a future growing in her womb and would do anything to protect it, *had* done anything to protect it.

Hunter walked her home, their silence an easy one.

As soon as they stepped into the house, he wrapped his arms around her. "I can't wait to see you grow round with our child."

She rolled her eyes. "You'll be okay with me being as big as a house? You're not a small man, you know. This baby could be huge."

Hunter knelt before her, lifted her shirt, and kissed her belly.

If she hadn't loved him with all her heart, right then, with that simple gesture, she'd have fallen harder.

She tangled her hand in his hair as he rested his head on her belly. "You know, I'd never been truly lucky before. I always tripped over things, ran into walls, had a shitty childhood. Then I found Dante, and I thought that maybe my luck had changed."

Hunter growled softly.

"I was wrong though. You made me lucky, Hunter. You made me see that I can be anything I want to be and have a future."

Hunter stood and helped her stand with him. She wrapped her arms around his waist and smiled. "I thought when I came back from hell, I'd have nothing. I thought I'd become the darkness that had threatened to consume me. You showed me the light, Becca. You saved me."

"You saved me first."

She cupped his face and kissed him, putting all her hopes and dreams into it.

Oh yes, she was lucky indeed.

A Note from Carrie Ann

Thank you so much for reading **An Unlucky Moon**! I'm so happy that you fell into the Dante's Circle world and found Hunter and Becca. I do hope if you liked this story, that you would please leave a review. Not only does a review spread the word to other readers, they let us authors know if you'd like to see more stories like this from us. I love hearing from readers and talking to them when I can. If you want to make sure you know what's coming next from me, you can sign up for my newsletter at www.CarrieAnnRyan.com or follow me on twitter at @CarrieAnnRyan. You guys are the reason I get to do what I do and I thank you.

Also, coming next in the Dante's Circle world is *His Choice*. This is a novella about Fawkes, the young demon you met in *Her Warriors' Three Wishes*, and Leslie, the submissive wolf you met in *An Unlucky Moon*. You'll be able to find this in the paranormal anthology *Ever After*. That's a brand new anthology with five new novellas that haven never been released before. In 2014, I will also be releasing Dante, Nadie, and Jace's book, *Tangled Innocence*. I've been enamored with the dragon since *Dust of My Wings* and I know a lot of my readers have felt the same.

Before that comes out though, I have my next Redwood Pack book, *Hidden Destiny*, coming out. It's time for North and Lexi to get a story, and let me tell you, I'm enjoying myself writing this one. There will also be another after the HEA novella featuring Jasper and Willow called *A Beta's Haven* coming out right before *Tangled Innocence*.

So yes, lots of goodies coming your way soon!

Thank you again for reading and I do hope to see you again.

Carrie Ann

About this Author

USA Today Bestselling Author Carrie Ann Ryan never thought she'd be a writer. Not really. No, she loved math and science and even went on to graduate school in chemistry. Yes, she read as a kid and devoured teen fiction and Harry Potter, but it wasn't until someone handed her a romance book in her late teens that she realized that there was something out there just for her. When another author suggested she use the voices in her head for good and not evil, The Redwood Pack and all her other stories were born.

Carrie Ann is a bestselling author of over twenty novels and novellas and has so much more on her mind (and on her spreadsheets *grins*) that she isn't planning on giving up her dream anytime soon.

www.CarrieAnnRyan.com

Also from this Author

Now Available:
Redwood Pack Series:

An Alpha's Path
A Taste for a Mate
Trinity Bound
A Night Away
Enforcer's Redemption
Blurred Expectations
Forgiveness
Shattered Emotions

Holiday, Montana Series:

Charmed Spirits
Santa's Executive
Finding Abigail
Her Lucky Love
Dreams of Ivory

Dante's Circle Series:

Dust of My Wings
Her Warriors' Three Wishes
An Unlucky Moon

Coming Soon:
Redwood Pack

Hidden Destiny
A Beta's Haven

Dante's Circle:

Ever After Anthology
Tangled Innocence

Made in the USA
Middletown, DE
23 July 2015